Raised by Wolves

by
Andrew Amster

Smudgeworks Press
Framingham, Massachusetts

Smudgeworks Press
6 Bancroft Circle
Framingham, MA 01701

You may contact the author at:
andrew@smudgeworks.com

This is a work of fiction. Names, characters, places, and incidents are either the product of the author's imagination or are used fictitiously. Any resemblance to actual persons, living or dead, events, or locales is entirely coincidental.

Cover photo & design by Andrew Amster

ISBN-13: 978-0-692-22689-6

Dedicated with love to Amy.
I told you I could finish something.

PROLOGUE

A child raised by a wolf does not become a wolf. Not an actual, literal wolf anyway. There are such things as genetics and chromosomes and inherited characteristics — all those concepts often taught with so little imagination in high school freshman biology. They do apply; they do have teeth. As for nurture, it can and does affect nature. It does not, however, put nature in a blender and change a nose into a snout. A snarl from your father at the breakfast table does not put fur on your brother's chest. Your mother's love won't make your breasts larger or allow you to sprout iridescent wings and flit about.

So if I tell you that this is the story of a Wolf Boy — perhaps even unintentionally the story of more than one human child raised by pairs or packs of animals once thought to be human but then demonstrably proven to be not quite so — you should know from the beginning that there are no actual wolves to be seen, smelled, or feared in the story. It's not that kind of story — and not that kind of wolves.

No. No werewolves either.

This story doesn't take place in a time when such things were more likely to happen than they are now. The mid-80s are not prehistory. As Ages go, they were less Dark, more poorly lit. Try to picture 1985 and 1986. What I'll describe happened before HIV/AIDS entered the general population. Of course, that didn't affect the wolves. These things happened before cellphones and the World Wide Web. A personal computer had five and a quarter-inch floppy drives and a 16-color monitor — that is, if you were truly cutting edge. The Internet was Compuserve on a noisy modem that tied up your only phone line. The lack of these modern conveniences did not inconvenience the wolves in any way. Music was still available for purchase on vinyl as well as cassette and eight-track tapes. CD players were still a couple of years away from becoming something everyone owned. The beat went on and the wolves did what wolves had always done.

The fact that I now have a daughter who is the same age that I was when this story takes place is not meant as either clever irony or eerie coincidence. I am purposely telling this story for her, even if I don't let her read it until she is much older or maybe until I am dead or until she accidentally finds it on the family's media server. I am telling the story because I think she should know these things I know, even if I'm not the one to tell her such things first hand.

The thing is, everyone always has been raised by wolves. What that makes me seems obvious.

So this both is and isn't the story of a Wolf Boy. Maybe you know him. He could be your father, your uncle, your teacher, your preacher, your upstairs neighbor, your county clerk. Then again, I have taught my daughter the politics of gender neutrality. So, he could be your mother or grandmother, too. Picture Granny howling at the moon if that helps set the mood.

It's just that kind of story.

CHAPTER 1

"Beth, do the girls at your school really wear clothes like that?"

My mother and I were sitting in our living room, watching *Murder, She Wrote* on television. A Cherry Coke commercial had just ended. In it, the girls were wearing wide-necked tops that fell off one shoulder. Another wore a tank top with suspenders. She didn't seem to notice the ridiculous things the boys were wearing. Parachute pants? Muscle shirts? Ugh.

I was finishing the last of my geometry homework for Monday. Geometric proofs were always about as mindless as network TV, so I was finding that the two things made a good match. It was late September of ninth grade and I was still feeling my way through my classes — getting to know the teachers, figuring out how much work I needed to do in which class. This one seemed under control.

"Not even. Mom, the girls at my school totally can't afford clothes like that."

What I didn't say to her was that every single girl I knew *would* wear whatever she saw in movies or on TV if she could and if the school administration wouldn't have a cow about it. We would all be wearing off-the-shoulder tops and bright neon leggings and stirrup pants. We would be wearing Guess or Gloria Vanderbilt jeans instead of the cheaper knockoff brands our moms agreed to pay for. We would have sunglasses and bracelets for every occasion. As it was, none of us in our town had that kind of money. We didn't have the money for the clothes and we definitely couldn't afford Hollywood hair. Most of us settled for a cheap mall haircut, maybe a perm, and then a hairbrush and an extra-large spray can of AquaNet. We had big hair and a tenth of the bracelets. That was as close as we could get to Hollywood glamor or being anything like the dancing girls in the Cherry Coke ad.

"It's just as well. It seems a little trashy to go around with your shoulder hanging out and your belly or bra straps showing. You shouldn't be allowed to do that at school." I loved my mom, but I wanted to roll my eyes. She always forgot in moments like these that I had seen a few photos of her — braless in her flimsy peasant blouses — back in 1968. I'm sure my grandmother must have just loved *that* look at the time.

"It's just fashion, Mom." I closed my math book and got up from my chair. "You want anything from the kitchen?"

"No, honey. I'll get up and get myself something to drink after Mrs. Fletcher uncovers the murderer."

5

She was sitting on the couch, knitting something large and orange. I had watched her work on this project for at least two months and I was still too put off by that yarn color to ask her what it was going to be. I certainly didn't want it to be anything for my bedroom.

I took my books into the kitchen and put them on the table next to my backpack. I wished I owned some of the clothes the girls wore on TV and in the movies. I could see myself in little black granny heels with frilly socks, red and black striped leggings, midriff top off both shoulders. I would walk into some club and the DJ would be playing *I'll Melt With You* by Modern English. I had Deborah Foreman dreams in an Ally Sheedy body. Well, a small town Pennsylvania Ally Sheedy. At least I had the hairbrush and my AquaNet.

The kitchen phone rang. I smiled. That would be my best friend, Kelly. We talked every night about this time. And if I knew her...

"What is it tonight? Physical science or your dad?" I said as I answered the phone. I didn't even bother with "Hello." Sometimes Kelly was just that predictable.

"Both!" she replied loudly then, trying hard to talk more softly, she repeated herself, "Both!" I could hear her fumbling with the phone, trying to cover her mouth. "He just wrote the check for Karen's fall semester. And so he had to tell us all at dinner how he didn't think she should even be going to college. That it's a waste of his money since she's a girl and she'll never finish. He's such a total tool!" She groaned. "It's not like he doesn't say the same thing — or worse — to Karen when she's home. But..."

Karen was Kelly's older sister. She was away at college. Their father, Gary Nash, was a local car dealer and a major jerk. Part of being Kelly's friend was having to listen to Mr. Nash stories. As Mr. Nash stories went, this one was about average. There had been worse. Much worse.

"And…?" I said, leaning back against the sink. I knew that, now that she had vented a little, Kelly would be anxious to change the subject.

"And I don't give a damn about orbitals and electron shells. I mean, I get it. I'm not an idiot. I wrote up the lab report and it's a great lab report. I did the problems and got all the answers. But duh. I just honestly don't care." She was laughing. I had to admit that the "Build-an-Atom" lab was the lamest one we had done yet.

"I'm surprised," I said with obvious sarcasm. "You were paying such close attention in class on Friday, too." This was not true at all. Kelly and I had the same physical science class and we sat together and were lab partners. (This was a beginning-of-the-year oversight by the teacher which he would rectify within the month.) We hadn't been able to pay attention to the teacher, Mr. Terhune, during the last ten minutes of Friday's lab because we were too busy watching one of the boys, Kyle Horton, trying to hide his uninvited, unruly erection from the two girls across the lab bench. "Clearly you care about some things in lab more than others."

"Shut up, Beth. You weren't exactly looking the other way, you know." I could picture Kelly at home, sitting on her twin bed, twirling the extra-long phone cord on her bright yellow Trimline phone. "Trollop." She laughed.

"Yep. I'm terribly loose. Always undressing the boys with my eyes." What would my mother think if she came into the kitchen and that was the only thing she heard?

"Beth?" Something had changed in her voice. She sounded serious.

"Yes, Kelly? What is it?"

"I have something I need to show you before school tomorrow." Kelly was talking more quietly yet sounded more excited than before. "I found something today that is going to blow your mind."

"And naturally, you have to tell me this now so that I won't be able to sleep tonight, wondering what it could be? Really? So nice. So nice."

Kelly laughed. "You know I am. Gotta run. I'll see you at school first thing in the morning. Mwah." She hung up. The line went silent, clicked, and then went to dial tone.

I hung up the phone on my end and poured myself a glass of apple cider. Ninth grade was proving to be much like eighth grade, except more so. Now everyone had hormones gushing out of their ears and eyeballs like open fire hydrants. Non-teens should only come near us if they're wearing those little rubber suits they use for handling hazardous materials. Toxic teens — a Superfund site in every school.

CHAPTER 2

"**W**here are we going?" I asked. Kelly had grabbed me by the backpack the next day as soon as I stepped off the morning bus.

"Mr. Witherow's room. I need to show you something awesome." Kelly often found things awesome. I thought it was awesome that I usually agreed with Kelly about how awesome things were.

"Is it an awesome rock?" I asked, smiling. Mr. Witherow had been our eighth grade earth science teacher the year before. And while Kelly liked the class and Mr. Witherow, she didn't care for the rocks and minerals unit. Kelly's answers on the rock identification test were along the lines of:

> **Sample 1:** <u>Rock</u>
>
> **Sample 2:** <u>Another rock</u>
>
> **Sample 3:** <u>Hard rock</u>

Luckily, she made a much better student of weather and climate, redeeming herself in the eyes of Mr. Witherow and the class science geeks, who were starting to worry that Kelly was just one more pretty face in stirrup pants.

"Yes, Beth. It's a rock. I love rocks sooo much, I'm naming my first child Dolomite."

"Technically, dolomite's a mineral, not a rock." She shot me a look. "You could simply name him Rocky, like in the movies."

"Stallone Rocky or *Rocky Horror* Rocky?"

"Definitely *Rocky Horror* Rocky! Born with fishnet stockings and ready to have sex with anyone or any thing that knocks on the mansion door."

"I don't think I want to give birth to anything wearing those heels. I'll probably have an epidural, so I won't even notice the fishnets."

"He could get his high heels for his first shoes, instead of those ugly flat, white baby shoes. Or you could have a C-section. Either way."

Laughing, Kelly grabbed my arm. "C'mon. Let's hurry! We don't have much time before the homeroom bell."

By this time, we were rounding the corner into the science hallway. At this time of year, it didn't smell any different than the other hallways. It wasn't until third trimester that the life science classes broke out the frogs and sharks for dissection. That's when the science hallway started to smell a bit like a mix of boy sweat and formaldehyde. That's also when it was possible — even likely— to find a dozen severed frog legs wandering the school, appearing on your textbook when your back was turned or lurking inside a desk in English along with the gum wrappers and ballpoint pen drawings of souped up cars. My mom told me high school biology was even worse when she was in school. Something about swarms of tiny, red-eyed fruit flies. But by the time I got to high school, biology was all chemistry and the only animals with red eyes were the stoners who hung out in the Orange hallway.

Mr. Witherow looked up what he was doing as we entered his classroom. "Hi, girls! What brings you here?" It was the beginning of the day. Mr. Witherow hadn't had time to get chalk dust on his dark pants yet. He was getting the plastic landform models out of the cabinet. It must have been time for the mapping unit. At 25 eighth graders per class maneuvering around 13 clear plastic shoeboxes filled with water, he should have been going to the janitor right then to borrow a mop for the day.

"Hi, Mr. Witherow! Beth and I need to look at one of the maps you showed us in class last year. You know? The one for the area around the school and the town?"

"You mean the USGS topographic maps? No problem. The one you want is in the top drawer over on the left there behind Beth. Mitchell Quadrangle."

Kelly opened the drawer and pulled out a copy of the map. As she spread it out on the lab bench, I happened to see Kenny Soto's name carved in the tabletop. What a dick. Why Kelly ever thought he was worth kissing was beyond me. He wore nothing but black t-shirts and listened to Slayer. I think that says it all. That he went on to become a balding Ace hardware "mulch man" was perhaps more giving the Devil his due than Kenny had in mind when he talked about Kelly and lied about her putting her hand in his pants. She didn't have to kick him in the balls; fate could handle it better and for keeps.

"OK, look. Here we are. The junior high. So that's Maple Street. That makes this street Elm and your neighborhood is over here. Your house would be about... there." She looked up from pointing to see whether or not I was following along. "If we go down to the end of your street and hang a left like so, that's my neighborhood. And there's where my house is, near the on ramp to the turnpike."

"Kelly, we looked at this last year. Is that it? Cuz if there's nothing to see here, I'd like to stop by my locker and check my hair."

"No! That's not what I wanted to show you!" She realized she was talking too loudly and that Mr. Witherow had looked up. She continued but, this time, just so I could hear. She pointed to a spot on the map. "This. This is what I wanted you to see."

I looked down to where she was pointing on the map. Beneath her finger was a triangular patch of green — a forest — located between the turnpike, the turnpike on ramp, and the north-south interstate. According to this map, it was a good sized forest. It was at least as big as my neighborhood, perhaps bigger.

"Seems like a waste to have that much land cut off from everything," I said, stating the obvious. "But, so what?"

"But that's it. That's what I wanted to show you. From the highway, you don't even notice it as you drive by. It's just trees. But here's this huge forest, cut off from everything. Just sitting there between the highways. It's like an island."

I still didn't get it. "But..."

We hadn't noticed Mr. Witherow walk up behind us. "So, how's physical science this year?" he asked. "Has Mr. Terhune shown you the Monkey Gun yet?"

"No, no Monkey Gun. Mr. Terhune still has us doing atoms and orbitals." I smiled. Teachers are often distracted by smiles. It makes them think you aren't going to steal the muffin from their desk or make up stories about them having affairs when there's a lull in lunchroom conversation. "Nothing to see here, Mr. Witherow" I thought to myself, not actually knowing what there *was* to see here. A hypothetical forest?

Kelly also smiled at Mr. Witherow, but I could tell from the way she edged into his personal space that she was going to level up. She wanted something. I also knew she was going to bite her lower lip and tilt her head a good half minute before she actually did. This move worked about equally well with over 40 married men as it did with 15 year old boys. Now all she needed to do was lean in another inch and ask…

"Mr. Witherow, do you have a spare copy of this map that Beth and I can borrow? We're trying to figure out the easiest bike route to the mall. And the street map in the back of the phonebook doesn't show the… topography like this map." I wondered if she had made that up on the spot or whether she had been planning to borrow the map all along.

"Sure, Kelly. You two can borrow that one, if you like." He turned and walked back to the cabinets. "But I need it back next week. I should be done with this contour mapping lab by then and then I'll have the kids looking at these quads. You remember."

"Oh, we'll get it back to you after the weekend. No problem."

Mr. Witherow also loaned us a cardboard tube so that we could roll up the map and carry it that way instead of folding it. He was a nice guy and a good teacher. I was a little sorry that we were using him a little bit, though I was sorrier that I still didn't know what this was all about. As we ran down the hall, away from his room, we made plans to meet at Kelly's house after school. Kelly promised me that all would be revealed.

"Hey, Nash. Gnarly hard-on!"

Yes, Kelly had the map tube between her legs as she was opening her locker. But still. What was Brian Briggs's problem? I scowled at him. Kelly took a more direct approach.

"You wanna lick it, Briggs?" That was Kelly's reply, complete with pointing to the tube and nodding an encouraging yes to Brian. We were so classy in those days and Kelly took no shit and no prisoners. Brian laughed nervously, looked around, and slunk away to draw boobs in the back of his Civics textbook, which I think was his main hobby.

CHAPTER 3

"So what's so special about this island-between-the-highways forest?" We were on Kelly's bed with the map and a bag of Ruffles spread out between us.

I always thought of Kelly's house as so much better than the house my mom and I lived in. The Nashes' house had a separate dining room; my mom and I ate in the kitchen. Their house had a separate den; our television was in the living room. But Kelly's bedroom was smaller than mine, even though her house was bigger. Her house had more — but smaller — bedrooms. Kelly and her little sister, Jenny, had their own rooms. Their big sister, Karen, was off at college, but she still had her own bedroom across the hall. Kelly's room was crammed full of just as much stuff as my room, but seemed to be fighting a losing battle against order. In a more confined volume, entropy was increasing. I wouldn't learn about gas laws until junior year, but something here probably applied. The change in temperature was almost always provided by Kelly's father, Mr. Nash. Speaking of entropy, I digress. My apologies. Back to Kelly. She was pointing at the map.

"Look at this, Beth. Tell me about this forest."

I took a deep breath. "Well, I guess it's some sort of state property. It looks like a screw up of some sort. This piece of land got cut off from the town when they built the last highway interchange. And that's about it."

"Do you think this forest would be a great place to hide?"

"What do you mean *hide*? Kelly, we are not running away again. Christmas is coming and I know for a fact that I'm getting a Walkman." Short story, really. We were young; we didn't get far because we only had two packs of Ring Dings. No one even missed us. The end.

"No, duh. We're not running away. Just play earth science nerd for a second and describe what you see."

I bent closer to the map. "Well, there's a stream running through the forest. The line is solid blue instead of dashed, so the stream must have water in it all year. And it looks like passes under this highway here and then under the turnpike up here. It's probably not big enough for them to build a bridge over it. So, the stream probably goes under the highways, through one of those concrete tunnel-things."

"Right. The stream passes under the highways. What else?" Kelly's eyes were big. It pleased her that I was agreeing with what she already thought or already knew.

"The land here isn't flat. These contour lines show that the elevations are higher over here on the north, get lower in the middle where the stream is, and then come back up again near the turnpike on ramp where it gets closest to our neighborhood."

"What about this area right here?" She pointed to a place in the middle of the forest. The map didn't show a clearing in the green, but the contour lines spread out, just north of a steep embankment and south of the stream.

"That looks like a flatter area. It has the stream on one side and then a steep hill rising up on the other side. But so what? Are you going to tell me what…?"

Kelly cut me off. "If you were going to build a house in these woods, where would you build it?"

"No place. There's no way to get the building supplies in. And once you got the house built, can you imagine the traffic noise between all of these highways? The noise is bad enough where we live and we're really only close to the on ramp. This place has to be a lot worse." I could tell she wasn't really listening, just waiting for me to finish. "Besides, I can't hammer a nail straight. My bird house in Industrial Arts looked like a parallelogram."

"Still. Right there." She said, pointing to the flatter area on the map again. "That's where you would build your house. A shack. No one could see you from the highways. The trees are too thick even without their leaves and this spot is way down in the stream valley. It's the perfect spot." She was smiling. If I knew that smile, she was finally getting close to telling me what this was all about.

"Except I wouldn't live there. I would have to have my groceries dropped in by planes. Except parachutes wouldn't work because there are all these trees. I wouldn't want to try carrying groceries through the concrete tunnel things. And I don't see any other way in or out of this forest. What person in his right mind would want to live there?"

"Right mind or not, someone does live right there. In that clearing by the stream. In a shack." She popped a potato chip in her mouth, crossed her arms, and smiled.

"How would you know, Kelly? You would have to have been there and there's no…"

"There is. There *is* a way in. I found it. A tunnel under the turnpike. I went through it, into the forest. And I saw this shack."

"When did you do this? And why wasn't I with you?" I leaned across the map and punched her. "You could have been hurt and no one would have ever found you!"

"Yesterday, after church. And I didn't get hurt. And I'm sorry you weren't with me. But… I found this place. And, more importantly, I found him." She smiled.

"Who?"

"Wolf Boy."

CHAPTER 4

"Wait. What? You found Wolf Boy? He's real?"

I realized that my mouth was hanging open in amazement, but I didn't care. Oh my god. If what Kelly said was true, it would be the most totally radical thing that had happened in my life — in either of our lives — ever.

You see, Wolf Boy was *the* local legend. Stories about Wolf Boy had been going around for at least 5 years, maybe even 10 years. And perhaps that wasn't long enough to make him a legend in the classical sense, but he was the most interesting bit of local color that my town had in the mid-1980s.

They called him Wolf Boy because everyone said he must be a boy raised by wolves, like Romulus and Remus. The fact that southern Pennsylvania didn't have an existing native wolf population never seemed to damage the story's reputation. Wolves, coyotes, rabid raccoons. It didn't matter. He was a wild boy, raised by wild things.

No one knew where Wolf Boy lived. The facts were that a shadowy, humanoid wisp had been observed several times a year, sneaking into town on moonless nights, stealing food and clothes and the occasional tool. And no, he wasn't just some boy sneaking around stealing. He ran like an animal — hunched over with this hands near the ground, almost running on all fours. Even so, he was faster than anyone who tried to chase him and he always managed to get away. Without fail, he would lope around the side of a house and simply vanish. It was even said that, when he was chased and got away, he taunted his pursuers by howling like a wolf. Or at least he made sounds like what *Punky Brewster*-watching suburbanites thought a wolf sounded like.

Not that he was actually observed even a fraction of the times he was thought to have roamed the neighborhoods. More often, he was the cool story that explained something out of place, something not quite right. A family would wake up on Saturday morning to find food missing from the kitchen and muddy human footprints on the kitchen floor. It must have been Wolf Boy. A gallon container of kerosene would go missing from the shed out back of the high school. It must have been Wolf Boy.

Even the girls who ran away to Pittsburgh or beyond for a week or two without leaving a note for their parents... the whispers would say they had been stolen away by Wolf Boy... that is, at least until they came slinking back home broke or called from their new boyfriend's parents' house in Allentown wanting money and their clothes sent on via UPS. But we all knew that Wolf Boy could have lured those girls into the dark if he wanted to. I couldn't think of a single girl who hadn't had a sexual fantasy about Wolf Boy. We thought he must be just the right part animal — hung like a racehorse and never burdened by having to wear braces on his teeth or go to Sunday school. Wolf Boy wouldn't fumble with a bra clasp; he would slice through the straps with his claws and pull the bra off with his teeth. And then we could be like him and never wear a goddamned bra again.

We all wanted Wolf Boy to be real. He was the perfect teen anti-hero. Someone needed to run free — and howl — for all of us.

"Yes, he's real. Or at least, there's a real guy living in the woods who must be the person we've all been calling Wolf Boy." Kelly was sitting cross-legged on the bed. She looked down at her knee and scratched at something that wasn't there.

I felt like I was going to hyperventilate. "Kelly, please! Tell me what happened, from the beginning. Don't leave out anything!" I pushed the map off the bed and onto the floor and scooted closer to her so that my knees were touching her knees. "How did you find the tunnel?"

"The better question is why someone hasn't found it before now. It's just back behind my street. You know how the backyards on my street all share a long fence? After that fence, there's a long clearing, then a band of trees that separates the clearing from the slope that goes up to the turnpike on-ramp? I know the neighborhood boys have played in that clearing for years. Brian, Kenny, and Eric Fuller all used to go back there to toss Frisbees and do their stupid daredevil stunts with their bikes."

Kelly looked up from her lap and saw the expression on my face. "I was mad at my dad, OK? I was back there looking for some bottles to break. I just needed to get away. I wasn't looking for the tunnel. I just found it." I knew better than to ask her directly about her dad. Mr. Nash had peculiar ideas about everything, particularly his daughters. Everything they did had to follow the plans he made for them in his head. Karen played along until she got to college. Kelly wasn't that good of an actress and never had the patience to wait for anything.

Kelly looked down at the map on the floor as she went on with the story. "Anyway, I don't know why the boys never saw this tunnel. It's behind the trees and overgrown with bushes and vines. But there's an opening behind the bushes. I mean, it was covered up with boards and pieces of sheet metal, but... if you see past those, there it is — a way into this tunnel. Five feet tall, maybe as wide as this bed is long. And it passes right under the highway and lets out at the edge of the forest on the other side."

"I don't know why I decided to go through the tunnel. It was early afternoon and there was enough light coming through the tunnel from the other side that I could see it was empty. It wasn't like it was a scary tunnel. It was dark, but not too dark. I could see the trees of this forest through the tunnel and they looked sort of peaceful. So I went through."

"What I didn't expect was that I would find a path on the *other* side of the tunnel. OK, maybe it isn't a path. But the tall grass is thinner or separated. It looked like it could be a path, so I took it. It's definitely the shortest way into the trees. I looked over my shoulder and could see cars driving by on the road above. One driver looked my way, so I know they could see me if they thought to look over. We'll have to run from the tunnel to the trees if we go back when it's daylight."

"Good idea. I don't think either of us is likely to look good in camouflage." I grabbed Kelly's pillow and put it in my lap. "Then what? You made it to the trees and…"

"The path actually is a path. It got clearer once I got into the trees. The forest is a mix of pines and… I don't know, maples I guess. More pines, I think. This path was covered with more pine needles than fallen leaves. The path started going downhill as soon as I entered the forest. Down and then a quick turn right. And when I looked back, not only couldn't I see the road or the tunnel any more, I couldn't even see where I had entered the forest. It made me a little nervous, so I told myself I would stick to the path and turn back if it disappeared or forked."

"The other interesting thing was how quiet it got once I was in the trees. I don't know if it's because of the trees or if it's because I was going down into that stream valley, but it got really quiet. You would think that this area would be noisy since it's surrounded by highways. But I barely heard anything— maybe one semi horn — the whole time. Again, I started getting a little spooked, so I walked more slowly and tried not to make any noise."

"I came to the stream, except it was a good twenty feet below me. The path just seemed to end at this steep drop off down to the stream. I was about to turn around and come back. I mean, right? I thought I'd seen everything there was to see. But for some reason, I took one more step, thinking maybe I could look straight down into the water or something. But what I saw was that the path kept going. Where I thought it ended, there was a large step down and then the path went straight off to the right. If you didn't know it was there, you might never see it."

"Like, I know it was stupid and I don't know for sure why I kept going, but I did. I figured the path must lead down to the stream. So I stepped down and slowly started walking. But I didn't go very far because that's when — boom, out of nowhere —I found I was looking down on this flat spot by the stream. You know, the one on the map? And on that flat spot of land was this shack, built back into the hillside. And standing out in front of the shack was a boy."

"Jesus, Kelly. Did he see you?"

"He didn't see me. I ducked back around the path as soon as I saw the shack and just stuck my head around the corner after that."

"What did he look like? Does he have fur?" I knew the last question was silly, but it amused me to think of Wolf Boy as Michael J. Fox in *Teen Wolf*. Kelly and I had seen that movie back in August and thought we wanted our werewolves a little less hairy. And maybe taller.

"That's just it. He didn't look all that unusual. I'm guessing he's maybe 16 or 17. Dark hair, tan. He wears clothes and they're in good shape even though they don't match. And he was standing up straight, not hunched over the way the stories go. He was just standing there with his eyes closed, sniffing the air. I just… Beth, I don't know why, but I knew this was Wolf Boy. It had to be! As soon as I thought that, I got scared. Duh, right? Maybe he could smell me, like my shampoo or my lip gloss or my *pussy* or something. So, there I am, freaking the fuck out. On the one hand, this has to be the coolest thing ever — but now I'm totally panicked. And as I turned to go back up the path, my foot snapped a stick or something on the path. I looked back to see if he had heard and… I guess he had. Because he wasn't there at any more."

"Oh, crap! What did you do?" I was hugging Kelly's pillow so tight to my chest that my arms shook. And even though Kelly was sitting there next to me — clearly not murdered — I was regretting having that second glass of Pepsi after school. I had to pee so badly. It was a nerves thing.

"I was still trying to be quiet, just in case he hadn't heard me, but I beat it back up the path. And I was planning to break into a run as soon as I stepped up at that drop off — you know, at the overlook over the stream? That step is about two feet tall. So I was looking at my right foot as I hauled myself up. And that's when I looked up and saw him standing there, right in front of me. Wolf Boy."

"No way! How did he get up there? How did he get up there that fast?" I suspect that I was rocking back and forth a little at this point. I had forgotten about needing to pee, but I was beyond excited.

"I don't know. Not only had he gotten up there that fast, I didn't hear him. And he wasn't even breathing hard. He was just standing there, blocking the path, maybe an arm's length away. He looked me up and down. And just as I started to say something, he stepped aside and pointed up the path. He was telling me to go. Which is what I did. I took off up the path and didn't look back until I was out of the trees. I don't know whether he followed me or not. I didn't see him again."

Chapter 4

"Oh, my god! You were that close to him! You didn't scream or anything?"

"No, I didn't. He didn't exactly scare me. He... surprised me, that's all. But Beth..." Kelly leaned closer and grabbed my hands in hers. "This guy is absolutely insanely gorgeous. I mean, he probably hasn't bathed in whenever. But... he's tall, dark hair, dark eyes. He's like Jake from *Sixteen Candles* without the decent haircut!"

The room was quiet for a moment. I raised my eyebrows and asked, "What now? Are you going to tell anyone else that you found him?"

Kelly shook her head. "I told you. No one else needs to know. He isn't harming anyone. And..."

Oh, here it comes. I knew that sound in her voice. I knew that look, too. Kelly had something in mind even before she showed me that map. "What? What are you thinking?"

"I'm thinking..." she said, grabbing the pillow from my lap and flopping down on the bed. "I'm thinking that you and I are going back to that forest this weekend."

CHAPTER 5

Just how and when Kelly and I were going to slip away and visit Wolf Boy Woods was left undecided. But then the opportunity was tossed at us like an underhand softball by my mother.

"Beth, do you think you could ask Kelly if you could sleep at her house this Friday night?"

It was Wednesday morning, before school. We were both in the kitchen. I was eating a bowl of Cheerios and banana, trying to give the appearance that I was in the kitchen with my mother before school, but truthfully either several hundred miles away (Jake, *Sixteen Candles*, somewhere near Chicago, I think) or at least half a mile away (Wolf Boy Woods, with Kelly and the real deal). Cheerios were the easiest thing to eat when you weren't concentrating. The worst thing that could happen was the spoon sliding past your mouth and getting milk in your hair. The hair had to be protected at all costs. Choosing the right clothes to wear to school took only a fraction of the time it took every morning to inflate my 1980s hair.

"What did you say, Mom?"

"I said that I have plans to go out this Friday night. I don't know when I'll be getting home and I would just feel better, you know, if you weren't here by yourself. So, do you think Kelly's family would mind if you spent the night over there with Kelly this Friday night?" She turned from the sink and smiled at me.

Oh, god. My mom has a date. "Um, sure. I'll ask Kelly when I see her before homeroom. She can check with Mrs. Nash when she gets home."

"Thank you, sweetie." She walked over and sat down at the kitchen table. "I can bake cookies for you to take with you. I bet little Jenny would like that."

"She'll have to pry them out of Kelly's and my hands, Mom."

Even then I wished there was something I could do to make things easier for my mother. Take that exchange in the kitchen, for example. I knew she was going on a date that Friday night. She could have just said so. By then, she was going on dates about once a month and, while she never let on to me that was where she was going, it was obvious simply by the extreme lengths she had to go to in order to *not* tell me where she was going or what she was doing and with whom. She was dating. What was the big deal about it that she couldn't tell me? Just because my Dad was dead? It's not like that hadn't been true my entire life.

More soldiers from Pennsylvania died in Vietnam than from any other state except for California and Texas. My Dad was one of those young men from Pennsylvania. He and my mother got married just before his first tour of duty. He grew up a couple of towns over. They had met through friends and dated during their senior year of high school. Then he got drafted. They quickly got married and my mother counted the days until he would come home. After 9 months, he did come home between his two required tours of duty. I was conceived, if not that first night then at some time during his brief time home. After he went back to Southeast Asia for that second tour, he lived just long enough to get my mother's letter saying that she was pregnant and that he should hurry home now that he was going to be a father. He wrote back immediately, promising to be careful, promising to be a good father, promising to love my mother more with each passing year. Then he got killed in a mortar attack somewhere in Cambodia.

That's what I'd always been told. I was born a few months after my dad's funeral. So I never knew my father at all. I have nothing to remember. I grew up with his photos and my mother's stories. I've been to my grandparents' house and I've seen his old room with his trophies and that sad, hardening baseball glove on the shelf. I wish I'd known him, so that I could honestly say I remember him and love him. But I don't and I can't. It was no different back then, when I was 14 years old, than it is now. Back then, I felt guilty about it. And I felt bad for my mom.

I don't think my mother dated at all before I reached junior high. When I was younger, I can't think of a single time when she left me with either set of grandparents that I didn't know exactly where she was and what she was doing. When she did start going out and not telling me about it, I didn't ask. We never discussed it.

Again, looking back, I wish there had been a way to make it easier for her. In our kitchen that morning, I knew that my mother thought she was probably going to have sex with this guy on Friday night. Otherwise, she wouldn't have made such a big deal about coming home late. She never brought anyone home. I knew that. But I also knew she was having sex. We only had one bathroom and one medicine chest. And those birth control pills on the top shelf weren't mine.

So I knew what this sleepover was about. And you know what? I didn't care. My father had been dead my entire life — almost 15 years. And while my mom loved him, that was no reason for her to sit inside and dry up like an unwatered plant. I grew up knowing that life is unpredictable at best, shitty at worst. Live today and appreciate the people you care about while you have them. That's all you can know for sure.

That much about life I got.

CHAPTER 6

I didn't see Kelly before school after all. My bus was late because of an accident and we didn't have any of the same classes that morning. I was finally able to talk to her at lunchtime while we were both in line, waiting to get a PB&J and milk.

"Sleep over? That's a great idea! Thank you, Mrs. Freeman!" Kelly was genuinely excited. "I know it won't be a problem with my folks. And…" She lowered her voice. "That'll give us a chance to get up early Saturday and zip through that tunnel before anyone knows we're up and gone."

"You mean it? We're going?" I never would have done it by myself, but the thought of going to the forest and possibly seeing Wolf Boy? With Kelly, it sounded like the best sort of adventure.

However, between now and then were all sorts of things that did not qualify as adventures. Classes.

Gym. And lunch periods. Kelly and I sat down at the table with a bunch of the other ninth grade girls.

"Well, I think Jeff Thompson is a great guy. I go over to his house after school some afternoons and he lets me do whatever I want to him." Cynthia Hale was between bites, trying to impress everyone with her experience with boys and boy parts.

"What do you mean, whatever you want?" asked Michelle Evans. She put down her forkful of macaroni and cheese.

"You know? Gaa. Like, play with him. He takes down his pants and lets me touch him."

"What a guy," Kelly said, barely keeping a straight face.

"Yep," I continued. "Quite a hardship for poor ol' Jeff." I hid a laugh behind my sandwich.

The other girls ignored us. I couldn't blame them. What Cynthia was saying was like having Moses bringing tablets of divine wisdom down from Mount Sinai. Cynthia had seen a penis. She had played with a penis. She knew the mystical ways of the penis. It was just a shame she was being such a dick about it.

"Did he...?" Lisa Jenkins tried to get this out without blushing, but failed miserably. "...you know?" She made an explosion motion with her hand. Yes, we knew what she meant.

Cynthia had everyone's attention now and she knew it. "Oh, yes. But not the first time. The first time I went over, I just played with watching it get bigger and smaller. And like, that's not as easy as it sounds with boys our age. Jeff was hard before his pants came down. I had him stand there so I could look at it. It stood straight out and it actually bobbed up and down with his heartbeat!" She laughed, looking around to gauge our reactions. "We had to watch TV for almost 20 minutes before it went down the first time. It got so small and wrinkly and silly looking. I didn't say that to him, of course. But as soon as I caught his eye, it started getting hard again. That didn't take any time at all. From this big to this big in 15 seconds."

"You actually touched it?" Michelle Evans looked at Cynthia over her glasses. "What was it… what are they like?"

"Soft. Hard. Warm. Pink with these veins below the skin and the head all shiny and purple."

"What else?" Michelle was going to be hungry in Geometry class later. She had barely touched her macaroni and cheese.

"The first time I made him come, it was an accident. I barely touched him. He apologized and was so upset. But I laughed about it and said I was flattered. The second time wasn't an accident. And I got to watch what happened. It went everywhere! And I looked at that and I looked at Jeff's face and I thought how totally awesome it was that I could do that. And then I did it again." Cynthia smiled at her plate, picked up her carton of milk, and took a slow sip through the straw. What a performance!

"It's not that special, Cynthia," Kelly said. "They all do it for themselves, a couple of times every night. You were like the left handed novelty wank for a right-handed guy."

Cynthia wasn't stunned, but she was clearly angry. "Well, maybe Kelly would like to tell us all about Kenny Soto's penis. By now we've all heard she had her hands on it this summer and didn't know what to do with it."

Kelly wiped her mouth with her napkin. Turning to Cynthia, she said, "Yes. I had my hand in Kenny's pants. Oddly enough though, I didn't find anything in there. Just hair and empty space. No dick at all. You know, I think Kenny may be a male impersonator." Kelly leaned forward slightly and spoke directly to Cynthia. "But really. If Kenny couldn't keep his mouth shut about nothing happening, what do you think Jeff is saying about you and your 'exploration time' to any boy who'll listen?"

But Kelly wasn't quite done. Picking up her tray, she turned to Cynthia and said, "Jeff's a slut. And you're just being a tool." She turned and walked away, leaving the other girls with their eyes wide and their mouths open.

"Let us know when Jeff offers to return the favor and play with yours," I said, rushing off to return my lunch tray and find Kelly.

CHAPTER 7

"Beth, could you pass that plate of leathery beef steak to me?"

By far, the biggest disadvantage to sleeping over at Kelly's house was having to endure even one minute at the Nash family dinner table. I always felt like excusing myself from the table so that I could set off a fire alarm or call the police to report a murder… anything to put an early end to the meal. We had only just sat down and I already felt my stomach lurching. And, despite what Mr. Nash was saying about the steak, it wasn't the food that was the problem. It was Mr. Nash.

"You would think as hard as I work and as much money as I bring home," he continued, "either we could afford to buy some better meat from Krogers or we might maybe get ourselves a better cook. Right? Right? Oh, Sandy. You know I love you." Mrs.

Nash smiled just a bit, but kept passing food all the same. "But look at this piece of meat. It's like the sole of an old boot." He picked a piece up with his fingers and banged it on his plate before putting it down next to his baked potato. "Jenny, pass me the ketch-up. Maybe I can soften it up. Or drown it." He laughed. He always thought he was being very funny.

The truth was, Gary Nash — Kelly's dad — was an asshole. I don't know why he was an asshole and Kelly was never able to tell me why. I take that back. Kelly never actually tried to tell me why because she didn't care why. Her dad was an asshole and Kelly was counting the days until she could leave this house and leave town like her sister, Karen.

Kelly and Karen both looked more like Sandy Nash when it came to their appearance. Mrs. Nash kept her hair back, but it was ash blonde like her two girls. Jenny had darker hair like her dad. But that may have been the limit of his similarities to any member of his family. I looked at him, sitting at the head of the table, and felt like I was watching a sit-com. Gary Nash had made himself look like the fool on prime time television — the incidental character all the other characters think is an idiot. The combed back hair, the whitened teeth, the ugly polyester pants and the too-wide collar shirts. And the tan. Mr. Nash was one of the first people any of us knew who went to a tanning salon. This was before the salons had time limits and eye protection. There were many times when I would see Kelly's father and his face would be so red that his eyes seemed to be like ping-pong balls glued to his face.

"So, Beth. How's it going for you in school this year? You doing OK in that physical science class?"

I never knew how to answer him in a way that didn't just lead to something. "It seems OK so far. Kelly and I both like physical science. We have that class together."

"And what's the math this year? Geometry?"

"Yes, sir. The geometry teacher is nice, but I think geometry is a little dry. Proofs and stuff." I was trying to stay off the subject of grades, but it wouldn't do any good.

"Well, Beth." Here it comes. I looked at Kelly and she was remashing her mashed potatoes. "I'm glad your classes seem OK to you. They never seem to be OK with *my* girls. I think school just doesn't agree with any of them. They just don't get the good grades other kids get. Look at Karen. Karen barely got through chemistry in high school. And Kelly here sure doesn't have much of a head for math." Mr. Nash waved his fork in the air as he spoke.

"Gary," Kelly's mother started to say. "Karen got a B in AP Chemistry. And Kelly is getting all A's and B's in her classes so far this year. I don't think…"

"No, you don't." And he laughed at that, while Kelly, Jenny, and I all just stared at our plates and tried hard to vanish. "Oh, honey. I'm just kidding."

But he wasn't kidding at all. He put a piece of meat in his mouth, chewed for a while, and then turned to Kelly. "I guess it's a good thing you and Jenny are so pretty, huh Kelly? You both get that from your mother. I guess someday someone will see whether or not either of you can learn how to cook a piece of meat."

I was sitting next to Kelly. I could feel her getting madder and madder. I could see her making white-knuckled fists in her lap beneath the table. If Mr.

Nash was like this in front of company, what was he like when it was just his family? According to Kelly, he had just gotten worse since Karen left for college. Not only was Karen not here to defend or at least support her sisters, but she wasn't there in the house to absorb the lion's share of the punishment. Now that was all falling on Mrs. Nash and Kelly.

Jenny, Kelly, and I helped Mrs. Nash clear the dinner dishes from the dining room. Mr. Nash had already disappeared to the garage. Kelly once told me she had no idea why he went to the garage every night after dinner. He didn't have a car to work on or woodworking to do. He just went out there and moved things around, put his unused tools in perfect order for some future project that never materialized. Kelly once said to me, "I'd understand it if he went out there and looked at *Penthouse* and jerked off. It would be gross, but I would understand it. But this is just weird." I couldn't imagine it and *really* didn't want to.

"Girls, you're welcome to join us. We're going to watch *Webster* at eight." Mrs. Nash was scraping food into the disposal.

"That's OK, Mom." Kelly put the leftover salad on the counter. "I think Beth and I will watch something on the little TV in your bedroom, if that's OK with you."

"No, no. That's not a problem." She started to load the dishwasher as we started out of the kitchen. "Just no snacking on my good bedspread! OK?"

"OK, Mom" answered Kelly, walking away. She turned and rolled her eyes at me. We both started to laugh. Kelly hated her parents' "good bedspread."

We let Jenny watch TV with us until eight o'clock. As Kelly changed the channels, she said, "I don't know, J. Looks like most of the shows Beth and I want to watch now might bore or scare you."

Jenny got the hint and sighed. "I'd rather watch *Webster* anyway," she said as she slid off the bed and quietly left the room. Jenny was in fourth grade and happened to be a really sweet kid. Even Kelly liked her. From what I had seen about having siblings, that was saying something.

After Jenny left, Kelly and I tried watching *Misfits of Science*. It was a new show. We had both seen one episode before this one. But after ten minutes, we decided that all the male actors in the show were way too old for their characters and the plot was beyond stupid. So we switched channels to watch the new *Twilight Zone*. We tuned in at the first commercial break, which meant we got in at the beginning of the second story segment in the show.

The story was called "Children's Zoo." The cute little girl in the story has these horrible parents. She receives a special invitation to come visit this Children's Zoo and somehow she convinces her parents to take her. When they get to the zoo — still fighting and being nasty to each other and the little girl — the parents are told that, like all the other children who visit the zoo, their daughter will see the zoo without them. They can wait for her in the waiting area. The parents grumble, but disappear behind a turnstile and through a door. The little girl is shown into a long hallway where a soothing voice announces over a loudspeaker, "To hear the parents speak, press the red button directly below the cage identification number." The little girl is not surprised by any of this. She clearly knew that this was what she would find at the Children's Zoo and calmly walks down the hallway, viewing different sets of parents on display. Parents who have all been abandoned for better parents by kids who have come to the zoo months or years before. Parents who either have or have not learned their lesson. At the end, the little girl chooses a pair of reformed parents and we see her original parents, trapped behind glass, watching her go and realizing that they are locked in and abandoned.

When the show went to commercial break, I said to Kelly, "Whoa. That was kinda creepy."

"I don't think it was creepy." I looked over at Kelly and she looked dead serious. "I'd drop my parents off in a second."

"Really? Both of them?" I understood why she might think that about Mr. Nash, but I didn't think she felt that way about her mother.

"Her, too. I'd push them both through the door and get a cotton candy before going in to choose another set of parents. Jenny could help." She was quiet for a second as she looked at the commercial without it registering. "Seems like a radical idea to me. Totally fine."

"Why your mom, too?"

"She's part of it. They're a team. You didn't see any unaccompanied parents in the zoo, did you? No, they come in pairs. I mean…" She realized what she was saying. "Unless one of them dies or something. Sorry, Beth. I didn't mean…"

"That's OK. Go on."

Kelly turned and looked at me. "I'm tired of her not trying to help things get better. It's her job to look out for us and she just doesn't. Ever. She doesn't even look out for herself. And I know I'm supposed to cut her some slack and think that maybe she's as much of a victim as me or Karen or Jenny, but... to hell with that. She's the grown up. She should at least try to make him stop. Really try. Not just 'Oh, Gary' this or that."

"Your dad is kinda abusive." I thought that was stating the obvious.

"That's for sure. But it's weird. I used to be mad at him 24 hours a day. I'm not anymore. He's just an unhappy, messed up man who wants to shit on everyone around him. To hell with him. I love my mom, but... I'm really, really mad at her. All the time."

"So... the zoo?" I offered.

"Oh, yeah. Definitely the zoo." Kelly smiled and turned off the TV. "Let's get some snacks and go to my room. We have to plan out our trip to Wolf Boy Woods in the morning."

CHAPTER 8

We were up, showered, and dressed early the next morning. We were anxious and excited. We couldn't wait to get through the tunnel and into Wolf Boy's forest. Of course, we also knew that getting an early start on our adventure minimized our chances of running into Kelly's dad and ruining our day. That part of the plan worked. Mr. Nash was nowhere to be seen. We did see Mrs. Nash briefly as we wolfed down some toast and orange juice.

"Good morning, girls!" Mrs. Nash said from the kitchen doorway, her arms full of dirty laundry. "Big plans for today?"

"No, nothing big," Kelly lied. "We're going to walk around a bit, then go down to the strip mall and see if the drugstore has Halloween candy marked down yet. We want to get a bag of Hershey bars to split." Kelly put our plates and cups in the sink.

"You two are really suffering over not being able to trick-or-treat, aren't you? Well, you know, I think the two of you had a pretty good run over the years. I remember that one year when Kelly, you were a Raggedy Ann, and little Beth was… oh, what was it again, Beth? Something from Disney, wasn't it?"

"No, mam. That wasn't a Disney princess. Just a princess from storybooks. I made her up."

"Well, I think that was a very good costume, Disney or not. Kelly's Raggedy Ann was a little too raggedy. I know Kelly's dad took photos that year and he said she looked like…"

Kelly knew where this was going and cut her mother off. "We're taking off, Mom. We're going to drop Beth's bag off at her house on our way to Rite-Aid." We were already halfway out the side door. "I should be back by three o'clock or so. Maybe four. OK? See you later!" Kelly grabbed me by the elbow and hustled me to and out the front door.

And we walked as quickly as we could down the driveway to the sidewalk, where we burst out laughing and took off down the street.

We did actually go to the strip mall. That part wasn't a lie. But we only went there because there was a Mister Donut at the strip mall and Kelly thought it would be a good idea to take Wolf Boy some donuts. "That way, he'll know we're friendly and mean him no harm." So we bought a dozen glazed donuts and a couple of cinnamon rolls for us to eat as we walked the long way back around to Kelly's neighborhood and the hidden tunnel.

"Have you thought about what Wolf Boy will do when he sees us? What if he's not there at all? What if he's left?" I was full of questions. When I stopped long enough to lick icing off my fingers, it gave Kelly the opportunity to answer some of them as best she could. The fact that they were unanswerable didn't stop her from answering no more than it had stopped me from asking.

"It's broad daylight. Don't you think he only leaves the forest after dark? That's the only time he's ever been spotted here in town, if that actually even was him they saw all those times. And…" Kelly took a bite of her cinnamon roll, chewed, and then continued. "…while I know me finding him and his shack probably upset him, I don't think it upset him enough to pick up everything and just move somewhere else. That shack isn't much, but it's his home."

"Do you think you coming back so soon and bringing another person will be too much for him? Shouldn't we just try to spy on him first?"

"Trust me, Beth. I'm surprised he didn't hear me coming last time. He'll know we're there. We'll never be quiet enough. And we smell like fresh shower gel."

"And cinnamon." I shifted my bag to my other hand. It was starting to get heavy.

We didn't see anyone when we cut through the Gillespies' backyard and crossed the clearing to the first set of trees. It was still early in the morning, but we were lucky that the weather had turned colder. The skies were gray and the neighborhood boys — the ones who ride their bikes back there — probably slept in. The first couple of months of school were taking their toll on everyone.

"Look! See those pieces of plywood? Last time I was here, there was only one piece covering the tunnel. And I know I was too excited to put it back when I came back through. He's been here! This must be how he usually has the tunnel covered." Kelly was already moving the sheets of plywood aside. I started to help.

The tunnel was as Kelly had described it: past the clearing, through the trees, just down the embankment from the on ramp. We knew we wouldn't be seen by the cars driving by above, at least not on this side of the tunnel. But, according to Kelly, we were going to need to run from the tunnel to the forest once we got to the other side. Drivers, particularly truck drivers, would be able to see us in that clearing.

We got the boards moved, stacking them neatly so that we could quickly put them back the way we had found them when we returned later. If Wolf Boy wanted the tunnel hidden, then so did we. I put my bag down just inside the tunnel. It was as safe there as it would have been on my back stoop at home. Briefly, I wondered if my mother was home yet and whether she had had a nice time last night.

"C'mon!" Kelly said, her voice quiet but excited. She was right to be quiet. It felt like anything someone said in that tunnel was probably magnified and hurled out into the forest on the other side like an announcement at halftime of the high school football games. So, quickly and without talking, we moved through the tunnel until we got to the other end.

"Where are we going? Exactly?" I was pressed against the tunnel wall, looking out across the clearing toward the trees. I thought I saw what passed for a path, but I wanted to make sure. Kelly could run fast when she wanted to and the last thing I wanted was for her to disappear and leave me stranded.

Kelly put her head near mine and pointed to a spot in the trees. "The path goes straight that way and then drops down with the slope. We go into the forest just below there."

"OK." I smiled. "And this guy didn't seem like the sort who would set booby-traps, trip wires... or dig one of those pits with spiky poles in the bottom?"

"No, but..." Kelly clutched the donut box and got ready to run. "No guarantees. Ready?"

"Always ready for an adventure. That's me." I wasn't nearly as brave without Kelly as I was with her. But I was with her.

Kelly counted. "We run on three. One, two... three." And we took off running.

CHAPTER 9

"You know, if he really was raised by wolves, I bet that sounded like a stampede."

I was breathing hard, standing on the path, just inside the trees on the forest side of the clearing. I think I was more excited than winded from the run. "He's probably down at his shack, thinking he can score buffalo for dinner." Kelly laughed. Looking out of the trees and up at the road, I saw a big UPS truck drive by. I could clearly see the driver. He might not have been able to see me there in the trees, but he definitely would have seen the two of us running across that clearing. "Kels, you were right about running." I pointed back to the clearing. "Drivers can definitely see down here if they happen to look this way."

Kelly opened the donut box. "It was a good thing we bought a dozen. They cram those in side-by-side, so they didn't get too shaken up." She tipped the box to show me and then closed it again. "Still with me?" I nodded. "OK, then. Let's do this!"

The forest and the path were just as Kelly had described them. There were a few maples mixed in, but mostly the forest was thick with the trunks of tall old pines. Short pine saplings were scattered along the forest floor, looking less lost than simply forgotten. There were the usual downed and rotting trees and moss covered rocks. Every few yards, patches of ferns, yellowed by the cooler autumn air, poked out of pine needles.

Once we got twenty feet into the forest and could no longer see the clearing, I realized that the car and truck sounds from the on ramp and the other highways had vanished. I heard the sound of a woodpecker knocking on a distant tree. But otherwise, it was unusually quiet there on the path. I found myself trying to walk more softly, trying to step on patches of brown pine needles because they made the least noise under my sneakers. I stepped over branches that might snap. Kelly was being the quietest I had ever known her. Normally, she made enough noise for five teens, three of them boys. Still, in spite of our best efforts, Kelly and I were clearly the noisiest things in the woods that Saturday morning in late October.

The more I walked, the more I thought that, even in summer with the sun directly overhead, sunlight would have a hard time filtering down to the forest floor. That morning, with the skies overcast, the path was lit, but poorly. It made me a little nervous. I had been on a thousand hikes through various woods with my mom or with friends in my life. These woods were darker than I expected them to be at that time of day. Everything seemed packed in, claustro-phobic. I kept looking from side to side, looking between the trees, looking for something that didn't belong there even less than we didn't belong there. At least we weren't wearing leg warmers or deely bobbers.

"How much farther?" I asked Kelly, as quietly as I could. She was walking three or four feet ahead of me. She slowed and stopped. Shifting the donut box to her left arm, she turned. She didn't say anything. She held up her right hand with the thumb and forefinger a few inches apart. "We're close then," I thought. And then she pointed up the path to where it seemed to go over a small hill. She made a diving motion with her hand. "That must be where the path drops down, overlooking the stream. That's where Wolf Boy caught her last time." I could feel my heart racing. I wish I'd had eaten something heavier than a cinnamon roll for breakfast, because my stomach was doing the Worm.

Slowly, we crept up to the place where the path dropped off. We stood there a minute, just grinning and making big "what-the-hell, are we crazy?" eyes at each other. This was really the point where we should turn back, if we were going to. And, to be honest, I probably would have, given half a chance. I was ready to jump out of my skin. And, to be honest, I didn't really need to see Wolf Boy. I had the town stories about him and then Kelly's description. That, by itself, would have been enough to fantasize about for a couple of years, if I didn't get a boyfriend first. Why ruin a good fantasy with reality? Reality probably had bad teeth and huge toenails.

Chapter 9

But I was Kelly's best friend and this was just
something we were going to do together. She needed
to go back again. And if she was going to go back,
then I would go back with her. In for a penny, in for
an epic disaster. Or the best time ever. It could go
either way with Kelly. So, when she handed me the
donuts and stepped over the path's edge, it never
occurred to me to stop her or abandon her. I simply
handed her down the donuts, took a deep breath, and
carefully stepped down.

CHAPTER 10

I've never been afraid of heights, but I have to admit that looking down at the stream below us made me a little anxious. I suppose it wasn't really the height that bothered me. It wasn't a cliff. The incline from the path down to the creek was steep, but nothing a person couldn't survive, even if she rolled down it headfirst. Unless she hit her head on a rock, of course. But there it was, the picture in my head of not just me, but both of us, face down and dead in the stream. They wouldn't find our bodies until Pennsylvania made the turnpike into six lanes and by then we would be nothing but bones and bracelets.

What I didn't want to wrestle with in my mind, right then and there, was that I wasn't really afraid of Kelly and me having simultaneous accidental deaths there in the forest. What was circling the ring, pawing at the air and not landing a takedown, was more along the lines of rape and murder. We would be Wolf Boy's deep woods bitches for a couple of weeks and then… Well, you couldn't expect him to steal or trap enough food for all three of us with winter coming. Again with the bones and bracelets.

We were both walking slowly and carefully. Kelly was a few feet ahead of me. I was trying hard to maintain a good distance. Not so far away as to lose sight of her, but not so close as to run into her if she were to stop suddenly. Which is what happened, not fifteen feet later.

Kelly rounded the corner where the path wrapped around the hillside. I lost sight of her for a few seconds max as she went behind the bend. I looked down at the stream, then down at my feet as I crept forward, and then, when I went to look up again, I was almost on top of Kelly, who had stopped in the middle of the path.

"Kelly!" I whispered. "Why are you stopping? Did you see…?" The next sound from my throat was much louder than a whisper and not under my control. It probably sounded like a bleat. It's the sound I imagine lambs make when they realize being sheared isn't the worst thing that can happen to them in life.

On the path, maybe ten feet in front of Kelly, crouched an angry looking boy dressed in worn, mismatched clothes. He was blocking our way and pointing back over our heads with one angrily jabbing hand. Wolf Boy did not want us there. He wanted us to leave. I could see his point. "Kelly, maybe we…"

But Kelly stood her ground. She had been scared by Wolf Boy once before. She was over the initial shock and was dead set on… I think that's when it occurred to me that I wasn't sure what Kelly actually wanted out of all this. We weren't there to capture Wolf Boy. We hadn't brought a camera to get his picture. What did she think would happen if we made it all the way to his shack? He picked up a large pine cone and cocked his arm to throw it at us.

"Don't you dare!" Kelly yelled, stomping one foot and holding the box of donuts to her belly. "I know you don't want anyone coming here and you're mad that I came back. And you're probably also mad that I brought Beth with me. Oh... she's Beth" she said, looking back at me. "And I'm Kelly, by the way. We assume you're the Wolf Boy. Do you mind if we call you that? That's what people in town call you, you know. Not that I really believe you were raised by wolves. We don't even really have wolves around here, do we? And besides, you're wearing clothes and a real wolf boy probably wouldn't bother with clothes." That may have been too much chatter, because a pine cone zipped past our heads.

"Hey! Stop it!" Wolf Boy picked up another pine cone and motioned for us to leave his forest immediately. Kelly wasn't giving up. "No! We don't want to leave! We just got here. And besides, we brought you these donuts. They're really good and god knows when you had any candy or desserts or anything. You clearly never got to trick-or-treat, right? Did you know kids in town dress up as Wolf Boy on Halloween? They're just making it up, since no one has ever really seen you. Mostly, they just put on ears and a black nose and howl a lot. You're not like that at all." The second pine cone was close enough to Kelly's face that she ducked. "Dammit! Would you please stop that?" This time, Wolf Boy picked up a rock.

"Kelly," I said quietly. "Let me try. Give me the donuts." I edged around her and she handed me the box of donuts. I opened the box. "This is probably very foolish," I thought to myself as I slowly started walking toward Wolf Boy.

Wolf Boy pulled back his arm to throw the rock at me, but he didn't. I made it a point to never look directly at him. I looked down at his feet as I crept forward. His feet weren't bare; he was wearing old boots of some sort. "We don't mean you any harm. We won't tell anyone else about you, ever." I spoke softly, counting each step a small success. "We don't want to hurt you or make you unhappy." I was close enough now that I could hear him breathing, see the skin of his stomach where his shirt wasn't buttoned all the way down. He was thin, but not malnourished.

Slowly, I squatted down and placed the open box of donuts a few inches in front of his feet. I tipped my head and looked up at him through my eyebrows, not daring catch his eyes completely. He was looking right at me. "We brought you these," I stammered. I looked back down at my feet and waited. When he didn't kick me, grab my hair, or smash my head with the rock, I slowly stood back up and backed away from him. He tossed the rock into the ferns and bent over to pick up the donuts. Then, without a word or another motion, he turned and walked down the path away from us.

"Oh my god," I said to Kelly, grabbing her shoulder. "That was so intense! I thought he might kill me right there!"

Kelly smiled, looking over my shoulder to where Wolf Boy had disappeared. "Beth Freeman, you are the bravest person I've ever met!"

"So, is that it? We should leave now, right?" I was more than willing to cut our losses and call that exchange with Wolf Boy my adventure for today. My heart was still racing and I needed to pee.

"No way," Kelly said, grabbing me and turning me around. "He's taken our donuts back to his shack. Let's follow him and see how close he lets us get."

"Kelly, what's your damage? He obviously doesn't want our company. He doesn't want *any* company. We should just leave. Let him enjoy his sugar in peace. Maybe I can get my mom to drive us to the mall or something."

"Christ, Beth. We've come this far. Don't wuss out on me now. You're the brave one, remember?" She started down the path, then turned. "C'mon! If we hurry, maybe he'll share the donuts with us. I'm hungry again."

"As if." But what I was really thinking was that we shouldn't follow Wolf Boy and expect hospitality. Nothing makes pelting girls with pine cones and rocks better than doing it while eating a dozen donuts. At least, that's what I imagined.

We found him sitting on the ground at the edge of the stream, maybe 20 feet from the entrance to his shack. He was eating the donuts, one after another. From the looks of the box, he had already finished nine or ten. He wasn't stuffing them in his face like Cookie Monster. He took bites. He chewed. But he didn't pause between bites or between donuts. He only paused to angrily look over at us as we entered the clearing. We weren't going to get any donuts.

"Don't crowd him, Kelly" I said, tugging on her sleeve. I pointed to a log a good distance away from

Wolf Boy. "Let's sit there. We can see him and he can see us." Kelly pursed her lips, but agreed. We sat down next to each other on the log and watched as Wolf Boy bit into the next to last donut. I heard the woodpecker again and wondered where it was. I looked around as we sat there, waiting.

A boy raised by wolves had not built this shack. Wolf Boy hadn't built this shack. From the outside, the shack appeared well constructed. This was clearly built by someone who knew what he was doing. And the shack wasn't new, by any means. It appeared weathered, but solid. I guessed that it was at least ten years old. So, when it was built, Wolf Boy must have been a little boy. I wondered if this truly was the only home he could remember or even the only home he had ever known.

The hardest part about building this shack must have been finding a way to secretly carry wood back into the forest. Maybe that didn't come through the tunnel? The shack had a metal pipe chimney, which meant he had either a fireplace or a stove. And since the shack was dug back into the hillside, it had the earth for insulation on three sides. That meant it was probably warmer in winter than I originally thought. I wondered how big it was inside.

"What are you thinking?" Kelly asked me, softly. We were both sitting there, side-by-side, our knees together and our hands in our jacket pockets.

"I was just thinking about his house. He didn't build it himself." Wolf Boy glanced over at us. He could hear us, even if we were talking softly.

"That's true. I guess I hadn't thought about that." Kelly was quiet for moment and then leaned over to whisper in my ear. "What I meant was what do you think about him? He's kinda hot for a forest dweller, don'tcha think?"

I smiled and nodded. Yes, he was hot. I hadn't expected his eyes to be blue. When Kelly said he had dark hair, I had just pictured him having dark eyes — brown with huge, carnivore pupils. But his eyes were more like a huskie — cold, but intelligent. He was tall, maybe five ten. Thin, but muscular. Not pale, but not tan either. His hands looked strong. He certainly wasn't anything like the boys at our junior high or even at the high school. It was like he was a different species. Not a wolf, but not a boy either.

Then again, I didn't feel like Kelly and I were his species either. There we sat with our big hair — Kelly with her perm and me with my feathered bangs — and there he was with his dark beard and long, dark hair he must just slice off with a knife. We had on our little acid-washed jean jackets and our acid-washed jeans (Unlike mine, Kelly's were actually Guess or Gloria Vanderbilt). His jeans had faded naturally to a blue that matched his eyes. The bottoms of the legs were tattering. He wore white socks with his old boots. We wore colorful layered socks with our Converse Chucks. He was wearing a long-sleeved, red plaid flannel shirt, partially unbuttoned. He didn't seem dirty. He didn't seem like someone who was living on squirrel and sleeping in the dirt. He was Wolf Boy but he didn't seem like a wolf boy.

Wolf Boy finished the last donut and stood up, cardboard box in hand. He started walking over to where we were sitting. So we stood up, nervously not knowing whether to retreat or stand our ground, whether to look him in the eye or not engage. Kelly looked him in the eye. I stared at his upper chest where his shirt collar was unbuttoned. He handed the donut box to Kelly and once again pointed to the path, clearly telling us it was time for us to leave.

Kelly seemed insulted. "What? You aren't even going to show us around your place? You know, we brought you donuts. You would think you might let us stay a little longer, show us a little hospitality…" Kelly was looking directly in his eyes, not backing down. I saw his eyes narrow and his jaw clench. I took that as a sign. "How about just showing us your favorite tree?"

"Kelly, let's not push our luck here. Let's go." I tugged on her arm. Reluctantly, she started to move. I looked back and Wolf Boy's eyes caught mine. His eyes were amazing. I quickly looked away — though probably not before smiling — and continued escorting Kelly and the empty donut box back up the path and away from the shack and Wolf Boy.

"We'll be back!" Kelly yelled to him over her shoulder. "Next time we're going to bring a whole bag of crullers and we're going to eat them all right in front of you. Do you even know what a cruller is? Well, they're good!" I looked back to see if he had picked up a pine cone to throw at her, but he had vanished.

"Crullers? Really?" And we both burst out laughing as hurried away.

CHAPTER 11

We discussed Wolf Boy all the way back through the woods. We had a million questions.

"Do you think he has a bed or does he sleep on a pile of straw?"

"Do you think his shack has a fireplace or a wood stove?"

"Why are his teeth so perfect when he clearly doesn't go to a dentist twice a year?"

"Do you think he wears underwear?"

"Do you think he *owns* underwear?"

"Do you think he's circumcised?" I'm not even sure why this question came to mind, but it made us both think. At that time, probably every single boy we knew was circumcised. And we didn't know *any* Jewish boys. It was standard practice for boys to get circumcised in the U.S. back then. But a wolf boy? Circumcision isn't the sort of thing that gets done in the woods. Maybe he would be more European in the foreskin department.

"You know he wasn't really raised by wolves, right?" I said to Kelly. "Someone who really knew how to use tools and work with wood built that shack. It wasn't him. He wasn't alone when he started living there. Right? Don't you think?" I decided I would research wolf boys when I had a chance the following week. This story isn't new. There must be reasons for the story to attach itself to a particular person or event.

After dashing back across the clearing, we continued to discuss him all through the tunnel and then continued as we stacked the plywood back up against the tunnel entrance the way we believed Wolf Boy wanted it to be. We were endlessly curious.

"I told you he was intense, didn't I?" Kelly prodded, wanting me to agree. "And darkly handsome?"

I wasn't going to disagree. On the other hand, I didn't want her to think I was all that taken with him. "Absolutely intense. And he has a good aim when he decides to throw something. I wonder if that's how he gets his squirrels for dinner?"

"Shut up, Beth. You're just trying to ruin it for me." Kelly folded up the donut box. We were at the clearing on the far side of the trees bordering the tunnel." Admit it. He's totally fascinating. I've got to know more about him."

I walked backwards ahead of her so that I could see her face as we walked and talked. "I admit that he's totally fascinating. You're right. He's made me curious. But, unlike you, I don't want to bear his pups." I ducked as Kelly tried to hit me with the donut box and missed.

"Bitch." Kelly sneered at me.
"Cow." I replied, wrinkling my face.
"Bitchy cow."
"Bovine bitch."

We were still laughing when we made it out to the street and turned down the sidewalk back toward the strip mall. Kelly had ditched the donut box in a garbage can next to one of the houses. We didn't think anyone saw us from the road when we were dashing from the forest to the tunnel. And we hadn't seen anyone near the tunnel when we were covering the tunnel entrance or when we were walking across the clearing behind the houses. For the first time that morning, we weren't worrying about running into someone. Of course, that's exactly when we did. I had to say I had mixed feelings about who it was.

Eric Fuller and Kenny Soto were riding their dirt bikes down the street when they saw us coming out from behind the houses and onto the sidewalk by the street. They came to a screeching stop at the curb. Trying to look cool on bikes they were rapidly out-growing, all they could muster to say to us was, "Hey, Kelly. Hey, Beth. What are you two up to? What were you doing back there in the field?"

After Kelly's lunchtime encounter with Cynthia the other day, I knew this wasn't going to be pretty. I wished I could have warned Eric so he would know what to expect. Kenny didn't need warning. He should have known what was coming. Kelly's eyes went narrow and cold.

"Well, look who it is," Kelly said. "Dickless Soto. I hear you've been telling anyone who'll listen what happened with you and me over the summer."

"Um, yeah," Kenny said. He ran his fingers through his short hair and looked at Eric for support. "I mean, I guess I may have said something about it to someone. I didn't mean for anyone to repeat it."

"Right. Maybe I won't mean anything by it when I mention to someone that I never did touch your fucking dick that day. That you came in your pants as soon as I touched your zipper and then you started crying. How's that for a story, Kenny? You think that might be a story people at school will think is worth telling and retelling? I do." Kelly gave Kenny's handlebars a hard shove.

"No, I…" Kenny looked at Eric, who was looking at me, his eyes wide. "Please don't say that to anyone. Besides, I just was going along with what you…" He stopped and reconsidered. "I'll tell Cynthia…"

"The truth? I don't think so. What I just said is the truth and you aren't likely to tell her that. So just shut up, Kenny. Just stay away from me and shut up. I hope no girl goes anywhere near your dick for another ten years. Asshole." She turned and walked briskly away. I shrugged my shoulders at Eric, turned and followed Kelly, proud to be her friend and happy not to have her as an enemy.

It was mid-afternoon when I got back home. I retrieved my sleepover bag from the back porch, walked around to the driveway, and went into the house through the side door. My mom was in the kitchen, deboning chicken for dinner. She looked up when I came in. "Oh, hello Beth dear. How was your sleepover?" It never occurred to her that, unless she had heard about other plans, I probably should have been home three or four hours ago.

"We had a good time," I said, dropping my bag on a kitchen chair and opening the refrigerator door. I took out an apple, bit into it, and started chewing. "That Mr. Nash is horrible though. I hate having dinner with Kelly when he's there."

"Beth, do you have to talk with your mouth full?" She turned back to the chicken. "Gary Nash has always been a little... oh, let's just say brusque. He rubs people the wrong way. But apparently he can sell cars like no one else. Why? Did he insult you?" She turned toward me, knife in hand.

"No, no. It's just creepy the way he talks about Kelly and Jenny and Mrs. Nash." My mom was wearing her blouse collar awfully high up. I smiled to myself. "So, Mom. How 'bout you? Did *you* have a good time last night?"

"It was OK. I went to see a movie and then stopped and had a beer with some friends. Nothing too exciting, I guess." She threw some chicken skin into the garbage.

"That isn't a hickey on your neck, is it Mom?" I took another bite of my apple.

"What? Oh, Beth. No. No, I just... pinched the skin somehow putting on my nightshirt last night. Hickey. Really? I don't even know why you know about such things." Her face was red. I supposed I should let it go at that. I didn't really want her to worry about what I thought.

"Mom?"

"Yes, Beth. What is it?"

"What do you know about Wolf Boy?" I sat down in one of the other kitchen chairs.

"Why do you ask?" She didn't turn around again. There were at least two more chicken breasts that needed deboning and my mother was never one to stop in the middle of something once she started.

"Oh, I just heard some folks talking and they were saying that some of the local elementary kids were going to go out trick-or-treating this week dressed as Wolf Boy. It got me thinking about it. Is Wolf Boy real or just our local town legend? And do you know anyone who has seen him, like for real?"

"No, no one I know has ever seen Wolf Boy. I've heard people talk about him, though. They say he only comes out in the middle of the night. There aren't all that many people who actually claim to have seen him. One of the deputy sheriffs said he saw Wolf Boy one night a few years ago, but the sheriff found out later that his deputy liked to do a little on-duty drinking, if you know what I mean. But yes, I guess Wolf Boy is our town legend. My friends who live in nearby towns don't have anything like it. The ones who live the closest have at least heard of him."

"So how do we even know he's real?" I got up and threw my apple core in the garbage. I leaned back against the counter, arms crossed. "Is it just that things disappear all the time? Like food and clothes?"

"I suppose that's part of it," she answered. She was almost done with the chicken. Growing up, I always admired how my mother could talk and cut things with a sharp knife at the same time without slicing her finger. I wouldn't develop that skill until my mid-twenties. "The police have taken finger-prints, so they know for sure that it's the same person almost every time something gets taken from inside a home. The clothes that get taken from clotheslines or from Goodwill bins? Who knows? I can tell you this. Maybe ten years ago, the police thought it was more than one person. The clothes that got stolen were for both a man and a boy. But then, maybe seven years ago, that changed. From then on, the clothes stolen were only for a boy. That's when people started calling him the Wolf Boy and blaming him for anything that happened."

"But why did they call him Wolf Boy if we don't have any wolves?"

"I guess it's from that expression: 'raised by wolves.' They're saying that he's been raised in the wild and must be wild himself."

"But mom, don't you think that if a person is stealing the town's food and clothing, he must not be all that wild? I mean, wouldn't a real wild boy eat berries and rabbits and wear clothes made from skins? Or wear no clothes at all?"

"You could be right, Beth. Maybe."

"Well, I think that, if whoever it is needs the food and the clothes enough to steal them in the middle of the night, I hope he's OK. It's hard enough being out here where it's safe and dry. It has to be a lot tougher being a wolf boy." I grabbed my bag from the chair and headed for the door to the living room. "Thanks for the story, Mom. I'm going to go take a shower and maybe read or draw some before dinner."

"Apricot chicken for dinner tonight! I'll call you when it's ready, unless you want to come down early and set the table."

I looked back into the kitchen from the doorway and saw her touching her neck. Definitely a hickey.

Later that night, after dinner, I was in my room reading *Flowers in the Attic* when I heard the telephone ring. The only phone was in the kitchen. My mom would answer it. She was either still in the kitchen, reading the newspaper, or she was in the living room watching *Golden Girls*. "Beth?" my mom called from down the hall. "Telephone. It's Kelly." Smiling, I put down my book and hopped off the bed.

"Hey, Kels. What's up?"

"I was just thinking…" Kelly said, something odd about her voice. "Does a Wolf Boy shit in the woods?" Click. She hung up. I laughed all the way back to my room.

CHAPTER 12

I woke up Sunday morning, determined to do some research on wild children. Wolf Boy wasn't a wolf boy at all, if you asked me. He wears boots. He eats donuts. He zips the zipper on his jeans. Whatever his story was, it didn't match the town myth.

After church, I told my mother I needed to do some work on a paper for Social Studies and had her drop me off at the Public Library. She was going to go home, change clothes, and then do the food shopping at the supermarket in the next town over. She said she would pick me up in two hours. That should be more than enough time, I thought.

Luckily, my favorite librarian was working the Reference Desk that afternoon. "Hi, Ms. Dornan! Do you have time to help me with something?" Judy Dornan didn't look the part of the librarian. She wasn't even 30 yet and recently married to one of the young dentists in the new medical building downtown. She was a redhead. Her clothes were stylish but not dull. I'd never known her to shush anyone ever. Not that I wanted to be a librarian, but Ms. Dornan was absolutely the best PR for the job there was.

"Good afternoon, Beth! Yes. I definitely have time to help you. What is it you're looking for today?" She smiled up at me from behind the desk.

I leaned over the desk a bit and lowered my voice. "I was wondering if you could point me in the right direction to find out about... wild children. Like Wolf Boy."

"Hmm. I bet we can find you something on that. Are you more interested in actual cases of wild children or wild children in works of fiction? Feral children have been appearing as characters in stories and folktales going back centuries."

"Feral children?" I interrupted her. "I don't know what those are."

"*Feral* is just another word for wild. A feral cat is one that is born to a mother cat without a home and then itself grows up without a home, eating whatever it can kill for itself, sleeping wherever it can find a warm place."

"Oh. I get it." I nodded. "You were saying that there are stories about feral children?"

"You probably have heard of some of them. There's the whole story of Romulus and Remus and the founding of Rome. They were twin baby brothers, raised by wolves. There's Tarzan. He was raised by the great apes after his parents died. And you remember Mowgli from *The Jungle Book*. Even Peter Pan was originally written to be about a boy who ran away and was raised in the wild by birds."

"What about real wild children? Has anyone actually ever found a real feral child? What was he or she like?" I didn't want my questions to sound too excited, but I was becoming more interested in putting a label on my own experience in the forest the day before. Was our Wolf Boy a wild child or not?

Ms. Dornan laughed. "Yes, I feel like every ten years or so, someone runs across a feral child and it gets reported in the news. Some turn out to be fakes, but there are others that seem to be real. Let's get you the *Readers Guide to Periodical Literature* and you can try to find articles. I'll go see if there are any books on the subject." She pushed back her chair and stood up.

"What about local newspaper articles on *our* Wolf Boy?" I thought it was worth a shot.

"I know *The Gazette* prints articles about Wolf Boy two or three times a year. But we don't have an index for *The Gazette*. You would either have to look through the back issues we have in the Periodical Room for the last couple of months or skim the back issues on microfilm."

"Oh," I frowned. "I don't have time for that today. My mom is picking me up in a little while. Maybe another time. For now, let's just stick to classic feral children."

I caught up with Kelly the next morning before school. My bus got to school maybe five minutes before hers every day, so I was always waiting for her when her bus arrived. It probably wouldn't be until after Thanksgiving before the principal and teachers would let us come inside the building before homeroom. This time of year, they expected us to wait outside once we were dropped off. Calmly, orderly freezing our toes off.

"Hey." Kelly wasn't wild about Mondays. Her shoelaces and bracelets might have been neon colored, but her face was colorless — well, aside from the lip gel and the blue eye shadow. She was wearing a black skirt with purple stirrup pants and one of her two jean jackets.

"He isn't really a wolf boy," I said to her, walking her away from the clusters of yawning teens so that we wouldn't be heard.

"What do you mean? We both know he's Wolf Boy. Duh."

I sighed. "No! I mean, yes! We met Wolf Boy. But our Wolf Boy isn't a wolf boy. He isn't really a wild child at all. Well, not entirely." I explained that I had been to the library and had done a little research on feral children. I explained what *feral* meant, just as Ms. Dornan had explained it to me.

"So here's what I'm thinking," I started. I had been trying to organize all of this in my head since yesterday. "Wild or feral children don't have any social skills. They don't talk. They don't understand words because they've never even been around language. It isn't that they haven't been taught words. They haven't even been exposed to words."

"They also are typically found eating things they find in the wild," I continued. "They don't wear clothes because they see no reason for clothes. Their feet are bare and covered in calluses. Sometimes they walk or run on all fours. If you were to go anywhere near a truly wild child, he would either run away or, if you cornered him, he would claw or bite you, trying to get away."

Kelly shifted her weight from one foot to the other. "The stories I've always heard about our local Wolf Boy say he runs on all fours."

"I heard those stories, too. But Kelly," I objected. "You've seen him now. Twice. For real. Yes, he's fast and he's quiet. But he stands and walks upright, just like us. And he wears boots with the shoelaces tied. And his pants zipper is zipped. You and I know boys here at school who can't manage that consistently."

"He didn't say anything to us, did he?" She looked a little annoyed. I was spoiling the Victorian romance of it all. "He doesn't talk."

"That doesn't mean he *can't* talk. Or, even if he can't talk, it doesn't mean he can't understand language. I got the impression he understood what we were saying, at least for the most part." I took a breath. "Look, Kelly. It doesn't change anything. He's still the town Wolf Boy. He's been out there in those woods by himself for a long, long time."

"So he wasn't raised by wolves?" Kelly asked.

"Kelly, you told me that you didn't think that was true. Besides, there aren't any wolves around here. The Pittsburgh Zoo doesn't even have wolves."

"Can we still call him Wolf Boy?" Kelly smiled.

"Yes, I said," taking her arm to walk inside. "Just not to his face."

CHAPTER 13

There was nothing more we could do about Wolf Boy that week. There was no way to try another trip to the woods until next weekend at the earliest. Luckily, life and school carried on as usual — and those were great killers of time. There was a lab report to write for science class due on Tuesday and then a big test in geometry on Wednesday. And then Thursday night was Halloween.

Against my better judgment, I said yes when Kelly asked me to come over and walk the neighborhood Halloween night with Jenny and her friend, Amanda. "C'mon, Beth. Can you imagine how ugly it would be if those two had to go out trick-or-treating with my dad? And if they go out with Amanda's parents, that means I'll be stuck at home listening to my dad answering the door and handing out candy. And we both know that'll be totally creepsville. So, do this with me. We can talk about the weekend and steal candy from babies."

I rang the doorbell and Mr. Nash answered the door. "Hi, Mr. Nash," I said.

"Beth! Aren't you supposed to say 'trick-or-treat?'" He was already amused with himself and he was only getting started. "But just what is this costume of yours? Sandy? Sandy! Could you come here and tell me what Beth is dressed up as?"

"I'm not dressed up as anything. I'm not trick-or-treating." I said it out loud, but he didn't notice.

Mrs. Nash did not come to the door, but Kelly came down the stairs, yelling for Jenny and Amanda to grab their bags and flashlights. I heard squeals from the living room. I remembered being that excited about Halloween. I also remembered liking candy corn. If we do knock over a kid later, I thought, we should leave him the candy corn.

"Oh, right! I remember now! You two are dressed up like the hookers from that movie, *Night Shift!* You know, the one with Shelly Long and Michael Keaton." He grinned at the little girls as they ducked under his arm and out the door. Jenny and Amanda had dressed as cats — one white, one black — and they were adorable. Kelly and I had decided to both wear skirts and leggings. Pretty normal stuff. Not exactly a prostitute level fashion statement.

"Funny, Dad. Maybe you just should let Mom answer the door from now on." Kelly let the storm door slam behind her as we walked down the sidewalk to the street.

"Wow. Your dad was a real douche tonight. What's up with that?" I offered Kelly a Snickers I had grabbed from the Halloween candy my mom was giving out back at my house.

"He's just like that." We came to the first house on the traditional neighborhood route. "Jenny! Amanda! We're going to stay out here on the sidewalk. You two can cut across the yards, if you want to. Just remember to say 'trick or treat' and 'thank you.' You get more candy that way." Parents would never give kids this kind of practical advice. "Go. Be free and greedy, my little kittens."

It was a good time to change the subject. "So…?" I started.

"So I think we need to go back to the woods this weekend and see if we can get Wolf Boy to let us inside his shack." Kelly took another bite of her Snickers. I had finished mine already.

"Inside his shack? Really? I love the way you jump from something easy to something hard in like one step." Having done all this research on feral children, I felt protective of Wolf Boy. And I know that made no sense, because I didn't really believe he was a feral child. But whatever he was, he had his reasons for wanting to be alone and living in the woods. I didn't want to rush him or force ourselves on him any more than we were already doing. "Don't you think simply going back and taking him some Charleston Chews or a warm jacket might be a better way to go?"

"We could do that, too." Kelly saw Jenny almost run into a hedge. "Jenny, use your flashlight!" She took my arm. "I just think we can answer a lot of the questions you have about Wolf Boy and his past if we can see inside that shack. Look, I know it seems like he doesn't want us there at all. But… maybe he does.

Maybe you're right and he hasn't always been by himself. If that's true, then he could be lonely. And we're good company, right?"

"Boundaries, Kelly Nash. Don't get in his face. OK? Deal?" I tried to look serious by looking at her through my eyebrows.

"Deal. Now, in honor of my douche Dad, let's practice our hooker walks." We both laughed as the Power Rangers and princesses and kittens parted before us like the Red Sea.

CHAPTER 14

"You don't think he could be vegetarian, do you?" Kelly asked me. "I'd hate to bring him a cheeseburger and him turn out to have zero interest in eating it."

Kelly was more nervous than her usual. We were about halfway through the tunnel. She had a bag of McDonalds food with her. I had a backpack with some socks she had taken from Mr. Nash's drawers ("He has thirty pairs, all exactly the same. He will never notice. If he does, he'll probably just accuse my mom of not keeping up with the laundry.") and a wool sweater that must have been my dad's. I found it in a plastic bag of clothes in my basement. I had mixed emotions about giving it away without my mother knowing. But, at the same time, I felt like that bag was more baggage than bag and that she should have passed that stuff on years ago. At least with my dad's old sweater, Wolf Boy might be a little warmer now that November was here and there was real snow in the weather forecast.

"No, I don't think he's a vegetarian." My voice echoed a little in the tunnel. "He clearly doesn't garden and there isn't much growing in the forest except pine trees, moss, and ferns. He couldn't steal vegetables from town in the winter. I think a hamburger is a better choice than Halloween candy." We were at the far end of the tunnel. I put the backpack on for the run across the clearing to the woods.

Since I knew where I was going this time, we took turns, each running as fast as we could. I went first. I sprinted to the trees, then turned around to look back. First, I checked the road to see if there were any cars or trucks stopped or slowing down. Nothing. Then I looked for Kelly, who raced across half a minute later. Again, I checked the road. A white car drove by, but it didn't slow down.

"All clear," I said, catching my breath. I took the backpack off. I preferred to just carry it by the straps anyway. We should have put the food in the backpack, but I didn't want the sweater to smell like a Big Mac and fries.

It was a few minutes after noon on the Saturday after Halloween. At first we wanted to tell our parents that we were going to the mall, but we realized that even if the story held up — that each girl's parent thought the other girl's parent was going to take us to the mall and bring us back — it might look suspicious for us to go to the mall and come back not having bought anything. When was the last time *that* happened? Even if it was just twist beads, we always bought something. What was the point of going otherwise? Being seen was only half the fun.

Instead, we decided to tell our parents that we were going to help Melissa Carr with an art project. They knew we both used to be friends with Melissa and it would make them happy to hear that we were seeing her again. The truth was, Melissa had started being homeschooled after elementary school and we couldn't stand being around her any more. We had nothing in common and her mother didn't like that we watched television and believed in evolution. It wasn't even Melissa's fault. We still liked her. But it was like she was living in Bora Bora, not the next street over. There was a great distance between Melissa and us and her mom's bullshit was the ocean.

Today the woods were brighter than last Saturday. The sky above the trees was blue and looked very pretty against the dark green pine needles in the trees above. I hadn't looked up last week when we were here. I was too busy being nervous about what or who was behind the trees. But now, looking up, I was impressed by how tall the pines were. These trees have been here a while. I stumbled on a root and stopped looking up. "Clumsy," I thought to myself, smiling. The rocks on the path were more obvious today. Many were covered with moss. Others were just dark gray masses sticking up out of the brown leaves and needles. The path wound through them.

Kelly and I talked as we walked, not trying to whisper this time. If Wolf Boy was going to be upset at us for coming back, he could meet us at the stream overlook and scowl at us there. Otherwise, he would definitely hear us coming and would need to either load up on rocks and pine cones to throw at us or else button his shirt. For once, we talked about everything but Wolf Boy.

He wasn't there when we got to the stream path. "Well, here goes," Kelly said as she stepped down and waited for me. "Let's see what kind of mood our non-feral child is in today."

To be clear, we didn't have a plan. We had food, socks, and a sweater. And Kelly had on a shirt with cleavage and more makeup than she probably should have had for an afternoon at Melissa's. I'm not sure that was part of a plan, but I didn't mention it to her. I knew I had spent more time on my own hair than I should have. I guess we both wanted him to notice us, to really see us. Kelly had her tits and her brava-do. I had... Well, I don't know what I had. I was somewhat of a work in progress. Maybe what I had was something only a wolf could see.

If he heard us coming — and he *must* have heard us coming — he didn't show any sign. We found him stacking firewood next to his shack. He turned, looked up, saw it was us, and then went back to what he was doing. I didn't see an axe, but I imagined that he had to have one here somewhere. The wood was in manageable pieces and some of it was clearly from much larger branches and trunks. How many winters has he been doing this, I wondered? He must know how much wood he needs to stack to make it through the cold months.

Kelly knew better than to expect him to greet us, yet she felt ignored just the same. "Hey, Wolf Boy. We brought you lunch." He didn't acknowledge what she'd said, but I felt he had heard it — and under-stood it — all the same.

"Kelly, maybe it would be nice if we called him something other than Wolf Boy. If he has a name, he isn't telling us. So… we should pick something. OK?" Again, I looked over to see if he was reacting to what I was saying. I know he heard me, but he showed no signs of understanding.

Kelly and I stopped about eight feet away from Wolf Boy. She lightly tossed the McDonalds bag up in the air and caught it. "I used to like the name Jason until all of these *Friday the 13th* movies. How about Jordan?"

"Mitchell?" I offered. "Alex?"

"Michael. Jeremy?" Kelly opened the bag, took out a cold French fry, and ate it.

"Daniel." I was looking right at him when I said that name and he looked up at me. He didn't change his expression, but at least that name seemed to get a response. Now, if only he didn't object. "Let's go with Daniel. That's a nice name." He didn't throw wood at me. "Can we call you Daniel?" He looked at me again. His eyes were clear, but sad.

"Kelly, why don't you give Daniel the food we brought?" I said, unzipping the backpack so that I could take out the sweater.

Kelly walked over to him and he stood up to face her. He was several inches taller than she was. He was dark to her light. His hair was straight and hers was a mess of 80s perm curls. He was quiet and she was Kelly. "Here." She handed him the open bag. "We brought you a burger and fries. If you don't know what those are, you're going to taste them and wonder why you're living in the forest."

Daniel sat down on the wood pile, looked inside the bag, sniffed, and began eating the French fries. After a few minutes, Kelly lost her patience and walked back to where he was. He stood up again, still holding the bag, staring at her. "You should eat the burger. The fries are better when they're warm but the Big Mac is probably still just as good." He wouldn't let go of the bag when she tried to take it, but she was able to reach inside, take out the Big Mac, and remove it from its wrapper. She showed it to him. He dropped the bag and took the Big Mac, which he ate much too quickly. He wiped his hands on his pants. Kelly muttered to herself that there were napkins in the bag.

I walked over to him. "Daniel, you remember us, right? I'm Beth." I patted myself on the chest. "And that's Kelly." Kelly waved, toeing the ground with one of her sneakers. "We were thinking that the weather is getting colder. I brought you this sweater. And Kelly brought you some socks. I know you have other ways of getting clothes, but... here." I handed him the sweater. I didn't feel I needed to get into how the sweater belonged to my dad and how he had died when he wasn't much older than Daniel was now. He looked at me and I thought I detected a slight nod of thanks. He walked over to the door to his shack and tossed the sweater somewhere inside.

"Aren't you going to ask us inside?" Kelly asked. Daniel looked at her, but did not acknowledge what she was saying. "Oh, c'mon. We figure you know what we're saying. You don't need to talk, if you don't want. I mean, Beth and I talk enough for twenty people." Kelly walked over to the shack and touched the outside. "Who built this? It's too old for you to have built it. You would have been too young. So who built it?"

Then, in the first sign we had seen that he really did understand what we were saying, Daniel pointed to a pile of rocks on the far side of the shack. It was long and narrow — just the right size to be the grave of an adult.

"Oh," said Kelly. "Your father? Brother? When did he die?"

Daniel didn't acknowledge these last questions. He went inside the shack, leaving us whispering to each other, wondering what to do. I picked up the McDonalds bag and wrapper, crumpled them up, and put them in my backpack. Now what?

We waited for what seemed like forever to us, though I'm sure it was probably no more than five minutes. "I'll go," I volunteered. Partly, I thought he trusted me more than he trusted Kelly. And partly, Kelly was as gentle as a concrete feather. If he threw me out, at least I wouldn't get mad at him and start yelling. She knew I was right.

The shack door had a tarp hanging down over it instead of a door. I knocked on the side. "Daniel? It's me, Beth. I want to say we're sorry if we upset you." I pulled the tarp aside slightly and looked inside. I saw Daniel sitting on the side of a bed. He was sitting up straight, staring ahead. He looked over at me. He didn't object when I pulled the tarp open a little wider and stepped inside.

I looked around. There actually was a door that could be shut and barred. The windows had shutters, also on the inside and with wooden latches. The floor was made of wood planks that were flat and even. There was a cast iron stove, not a fireplace, hooked up to that chimney I had seen. There was a table with two chairs. There was what must have been a bed in the far corner of the room, covered with tools and clothes. And then there was the bed Daniel was sitting on. You couldn't tell the room was half buried in the hillside. But it was a bit earthy smelling and quiet. I could hear Daniel breathing as he watched me look over his home.

I tried not to look at him as I spoke, but couldn't help myself. "This is nice. Whoever built this did a very nice job with it. It must have been really hard building something like this so far into these woods." He looked at me, past me, then at me again. Whoever it was, he missed them a lot.

"Daniel, will you let me ask Kelly inside? Just for a second. If you let her come in and see, I promise you she'll be quiet. She'll just look around like I just did and then she and I will pack up and leave you alone." This was risky for several reasons, but I figured it was my best shot at getting Kelly what she wanted — at least the part she acknowledged wanting — and not causing Wolf Boy any more anxiety for one day. I was guessing he knew we would be back. He looked down at the floor. "That's an OK then? Right? I'm going to step outside and tell Kelly she can come inside." Again, I took the lack of *no* for a *yes*. I backed out the door.

Kelly had been listening outside. I gave her the wide-eyed, "Take this seriously!" look. "Kelly," I whispered. "Make this fast and don't make waves. It's his home. If we don't mess this up, he'll let us come back. OK?"

"OK, OK," she replied, as if she knew it all along. Then she followed me inside.

Less than half an hour later, we had made our way back at the edge of the forest. Kelly had barely spoken inside Daniel's shack. It went quickly. We soon told Daniel goodbye, gathered our belongings, and started up the path for home. I looked back and saw Daniel standing at his door, watching us walk up the path.

We stood looking across the clearing. The tunnel was up and over the rise. A large truck drove by on the highway. We could see the driver. We ducked back behind the trees, but he never looked over our way as he accelerated up the on ramp.

"Kelly," I said, straightening up. "It's going to snow soon. How are we going to make it back and forth across this clearing without leaving tracks?"

CHAPTER 15

November began to get away from us. The weather got colder and the days seemed even shorter once daylight savings time ended. The nights seemed long and claustrophobic — and Kelly and I both knew it would only get worse when winter finally did arrive. The teachers at school assigned the first actual long-term projects of the school year. For the classes without papers or projects, such as geometry, they increased the number of problems we had to do each week. I suppose they didn't want to seem less important, less deserving of our time at home than the classes with projects. School had gone from being a drag to being a grind.

Our families also started demanding more of our time. November meant Thanksgiving and that meant Christmas was coming. In those days, newspapers counted down the shopping days until Christmas on the front page. So weekend trips to the mall became a regular, mandatory thing. Nothing says *family* like shopping for five hours and buying next to nothing, over and over again.

The next weekend was a three-day weekend because Veterans Day fell on a Monday that year. Kelly and I were both tied up with families on both Saturday and Sunday. She was free on Monday and really wanted for us to go see Wolf Boy then. But I unfortunately had other plans. I had to take part in an uncomfortable Veterans Day family tradition.

My grandparents, my mother, and I got back to my grandparents' house a little bit before noon. My grandmother quietly took off her coat, hung it in the closet, and started putting cold cuts, mustard, and other sandwich makings on the dining room table. This is what she did every year when we got back from the cemetery.

Standing at the cemetery with my grandfather, watching Gram and my mother put flowers on my father's grave, for the first time in my life I was aware that we should have been doing this in May on Memorial Day. It would have been spring then and the trees would have just gotten their leaves. The grass would have been green and flowers in the cemetery would have been blooming. But no. My family chooses to come out to the cemetery when the trees are bare, the grass browning, and the spring birds already back in Florida. As if cemeteries weren't depressing enough. Some people need to wallow. Some people need to hold on to their suffering as much as they need to hold on to the person they've lost. That was my Gram.

"Beth, could you pass the ham this way, please?" Grampa smiled at me and thanked me as I passed the ham and then the mustard his way. "How's school? Are the teachers getting you ready for high school next year?"

"I guess. They give us a lot more work in ninth grade than they did in eighth grade." I took a bite of my sandwich.

"What's your favorite class this year?" Grampa asked, still making his sandwich. My mother had taken one bite, but didn't seem very hungry. Gram was looking off somewhere. She hadn't put anything on her plate at all.

"Geometry, I guess. I mean, I don't like having to do so many of these proofs and how the teacher won't let me skip steps even when I know how it works. But I feel pretty good about it when I get them finished and they're right." And that was true. Geometry was growing on me. The step-by-step logic of geometric proofs made me happy. If you just followed the rules, the outcome was predictable, inevitable, and true.

"Beth, your father was so good at math when he was your age," Gram started. "I remember him sitting at this table doing his algebra problems in high school. I would try to look over his shoulder but he would shoo me away or ask me to get him a glass of milk. Ben sure did love to drink milk."

It would go on like this all afternoon. My grandfather, mother, and I would try to have conversations about 1985. And my grandmother would always turn everything back to 1965, 1968, or 1970. The silences between attempts would get longer and longer until my mother would suddenly jump up and announce it was time for us to drive home. Gram would say goodbye and go into Ben's old bedroom and sit on his bed. Grampa would shrug his shoulders, sigh, and sadly hug us both goodbye.

There was one more Veterans Day tradition in my family. When my mother and I got home that afternoon, she poured herself some bourbon in a tumbler of ice, went to her bedroom, and closed the door. When she didn't reappear by dinnertime, I made myself a PB&J and went back to my room to review for Tuesday's physical science test. I turned on the radio and kept the volume low. Madonna. Katrina and the Waves. Duran Duran. I didn't care what the DJ played as long as it sounded like any other day.

CHAPTER 16

So it was two weeks before Kelly and I were able to make up an excuse, ditch our families, and go back to the forest to see Daniel. This time we took him an Arby's roast beef sandwich and a pair of long underwear Kelly had stolen from her uncle. "He has like ten of these things. He's not going to miss one pair." Kelly's uncle liked to ice fish in Minnesota. So it stood to reason he might have a few pairs of long underwear.

Daniel came out of his shack as we were coming down the stream trail. We weren't getting any quieter, I suppose. He tipped his head a bit when Kelly handed him the Arby's bag and he let us come inside his shack where it was warm. The stove was lit and inside the shack was surprisingly comfortable.

Kelly and I sat side-by-side on his bed while Daniel sat at the table, eating the sandwich. The bed's mattress was simple. It reminded me of the futon at my cousin's house, but thinner. The blankets were plain and wool. If there had ever been sheets, those had long since worn out and been reused as rags. The pillow had no pillowcase and was leaking feathers. I told myself to bring Daniel a pillowcase the next time I came.

As he ate, Kelly and I babbled. We spoke to him about things he probably didn't care about. We spoke to each other as if he wasn't there. Kelly asked Daniel questions that she and I both knew he wouldn't answer. He looked at us through his hair as he chewed. Finally I arrived at a question that did seem worth his attention.

"Daniel," I started. "We know you want to keep it a secret that you're living out here. And Kelly and I have been really careful about putting the boards back over the tunnel whenever we go through, just the way you want them. But it's going to snow soon. What do you want us to do? We don't know how to get here without leaving tracks in the snow that people might see from the road." Daniel got up from the table and put the empty Arby's wrapper and bag into the stove where they quickly flamed and sizzled. He went back over and sat back down on the chair, bolt upright, looking straight at me. "So... I mean, Kelly and I want to keep coming here, if that's OK with you. Once it snows, is there some other way we could get here that won't be so obvious?"

His eyes did not stop staring into mine as he nodded. Kelly's mouth popped open with surprise. "So you *do* understand everything we say!" He got up and walked over to the shack door. He looked back at us and then went outside.

"C'mon, Kelly. He wants to show us something!"

Daniel walked around the mound of rocks — the one we assumed was a grave — and up a path on the far side. We followed him, single file. The trail was similar to the one on the other side. It went up and wound its way to the right, bearing over toward the edge of the woods and the turnpike on ramp.

Daniel motioned for me to come closer. I stood next to him as he pointed out of the trees toward what should have been the clearing. The space between the forest and the road was much narrower here than it was at the tunnel. The slope up to the road was maybe ten feet away. I could see that embankment and the clearing both stretched on for a long ways to my right.

"How does this help us not leave footprints in the snow?"

Daniel stepped out of the trees toward the embankment. Then he walked carefully along the place where the slope changed — the place where the embankment intersected the flatter clearing. He walked four feet, stopped, then made a motion with his arm that indicated we should continue on like that. He turned around and came back to where we were waiting in the trees.

"Oh! If we walk there, then it doesn't matter if we leave footprints. No one will see them. Drivers looking out their windows only see the clearing, not the slope down to the clearing. That's great! And the tunnel is just up there, isn't it?"

Daniel nodded for the second time that day. He looked over at Kelly who had moved very close to him. He stepped back a little, then turned to go back to his shack.

Chapter 16

"Let's go, Kelly. That's enough for one day." I knew she wanted to follow him, just as I knew it would be a bad idea. Take the small victories. Don't push your luck. Follow the steps.

"Aww. Can't we go help him try on his Long Johns?" She grinned. She knew I was thinking the same thing and it annoyed me.

"Perv," I called her, leading her out of the woods and along the slope break toward the tunnel.

"Other perv," she replied.

CHAPTER 17

Sure enough, it snowed several inches that Tuesday. It wasn't enough snow to call off school and it was barely enough for the young guys in their baseball caps and flannel shirts to finally attach the plows to their pick-up trucks for the next several months, but it snowed. It was still a week before Thanksgiving and psychological winter had already begun. My mom had shoveled our driveway by the time I got up to go to school that day. I shoveled the sidewalk in front of the house when I got home. Kelly's dad usually hired one of the neighborhood boys to shovel theirs.

So, in spite of the snow, Kelly and I were able to go visit Daniel one more time before Thanksgiving. As much as we thought it would be nice to bring Daniel Thanksgiving leftovers, we knew that wouldn't be possible. And since Thanksgiving was on the 28th this year, we wouldn't be able to come back to the woods again until December. We explained that to Daniel as we said goodbye. I wondered whether time seemed shorter to him or longer. Would he miss us?

For me and my mom, Thanksgiving was the nicest holiday of the year. We always went to my other grandparents' — my mom's parents — house for Thanksgiving. I would get up at about eight o'clock on Thanksgiving Day. We would turn on the television and watch the Macy's parade from New York while we peeled and cut up the potatoes for mashed potatoes. We always took the potatoes for the mashed potatoes. We would cook them before we left and then mash them when we got to Gramma and Grampa's house. The big dinner was always early, around one in the afternoon.

It wasn't surprising that I always looked forward to Thanksgiving. For one thing, I just liked Thanksgiving food better than food for all the other holidays. Turkey, stuffing, mashed potatoes — and lots of gravy. And then more pies and desserts than should possibly fit on one sideboard.

The other thing I liked about Thanksgiving was seeing my mother laughing and having a good time. Her two sisters would be there with my uncles and all my cousins. Some years, there were as many as 30 people at my grandparents' for dinner. It was loud and funny and chaotic — and it didn't have anything to do with Jesus and all that baggage. It was just food and family. And that suited me and my mother just fine.

Thanksgiving wasn't as warm and fuzzy at the Nash house. Their Thanksgiving dinner was just the immediate family — Mr. and Mrs. Nash, Kelly, Jenny, and Karen. And it never went well. I knew this because

I'd gotten Thanksgiving night phone calls from Kelly for several years now. So I wasn't surprised when Kelly called me after I got home that evening. Her big dinner had just ended and she needed to blow off steam.

"You would not *believe* what I just sat through," Kelly started. But, Kelly was wrong about that. Having sat through regular dinners with the Nashes, I would believe just about anything she was going to tell me. Mr. Nash was nothing if not predictably awful and... well, Kelly's sister Karen didn't just sit there and take it anymore. There were bound to be more fireworks this year than last.

I hopped up on the kitchen counter and sat with my legs dangling off. I figured I should make myself comfortable. "What happened this time? Food fight?" It didn't matter what I said or asked. The story was going to come out the way Kelly wanted to tell it.

"Forget that he insulted my mother's cooking when she did the whole dinner by herself, including the shopping, without any help from him. I mean, that's bad, but that's their usual bullshit. He insults her and her cooking and she lets him. But that was nothing. That was like the asshole appetizer."

I cared about Kelly's story, but I was also starting to think I was might finally be getting hungry enough to have a piece of leftover apple pie. I thought I would help her get to the point. "So I assume your Dad and Karen got into it? What happened?"

"First, he asked her about college. Everyone at the table knew he was only asking so that he could tell her that she was wasting his money and that getting a teaching degree was stupid... which, of course, he did. Then Karen told him that she won't need his money much longer and that he should be a little happier that she gets grants and works a part time job while she's at school. But he wouldn't let it go. He said she was being stupid for getting a degree when all she was going to do was get married anyway. But then, Karen said, 'Yes, Dad. All I want out of life is the perfect marriage you and Mom have.' I thought he was going to choke on his turkey. His face turned so red."

"Did she mean anything by that or just…?"

"I don't know. I really don't know. But it got nastier after that until Karen finally threw her napkin on the table and left the room. It was awful. My mother started crying and my dad actually told her to stop. Karen came back a little later after my dad went to the den to watch TV to help me and Mom clean up and put things away. No one said a word to one another the whole time. Beth, the whole thing was seriously screwed up. I mean it. Even by our standards. It's a wonder Karen comes home at all."

"How about Jenny? Is she OK?"

Kelly sighed. "Pffft. I want to think so, but… I don't know. This stuff didn't go over *my* head when I was her age, right? She may not be talking about it to Mom or to me, but I bet you heard some of it from me when I was her age."

"Yeah, a little. More as we got older." I didn't say so, but I remembered. It was harder for Kelly to talk about her parents back then.

"I'm thinking Jenny is just keeping a low profile. I should spend more time with her… see if she needs to talk. Not that I know what to say to her. 'Gosh, kid. Sorry, but our father's a piece of…'"

I interrupted her. "Have you talked to Karen?"

"No, she went out with some of her old high school friends for the night. If she's smart, she's making plans to stay out the rest of the time she's home. That's what I would do, if I were her."

"When does she go back to school?"

"She has a ride back early Sunday afternoon." Kelly paused, then shifted topics. "So… how many pies at your family's soiree this year? Did you kiss any cousins? Did your uncles all have their belts unbuckled while they watched the football game?"

"Of course they did. That's the American way. You know that." The crisis had passed. I was definitely having leftover apple pie. With vanilla ice cream. That's also the American way.

I spent Black Friday with my mother at the mall. I was exhausted by the time we made it home with only a few bags of Christmas presents successfully chosen and purchased at supposedly bargain prices. By Saturday afternoon, the last thing I wanted to do was any more shopping. And since it was still officially part of the Thanksgiving holiday weekend, I had no interest in working on anything for school. So instead of going to a different mall with my mother, I accepted Kelly's invitation to come over to her house and do each other's nails. We were both hoping my presence would reduce the tension in the Nash house, although it had never done that before. I suppose, to Gary Nash, I was simply the daughter he hadn't been nasty to yet.

We had been in Kelly's room with the window cracked for a couple of hours when Karen walked in, shut the door, and flopped down on the bed. She was wearing her coat. Kelly and I were sitting cross-legged on the floor, waving our hands slowly and trying to think of the perfect Christmas present for a Wolf Boy that wasn't a Wolf Girl.

"Our father is a prick," Karen announced to the ceiling.

"You knew that before you got two years of college education." Kelly looked admiringly at the red metal flake nail polish on her fingernails. I had talked her out of neon green. "He hasn't gotten any better since you've been away, in case you were wondering."

"I didn't think he would. He's a natural asshole. And a misogynist."

"And that means…what?" Kelly asked, rolling her eyes at me. I already knew what it meant.

"It means he's a man with a wife and three daughters who just so happens to hate women. He's mean and petty and impossible to be around."

Kelly turned to look at Karen. "So you're not around. Lucky you." She didn't sound like she was happy for Karen and Karen noticed.

"Sis, your time will come. You and Jenny will get out of here, too. Mom's the one who's really stuck. Just stay out of his way and don't get into it with him. It doesn't do any good." Karen had turned over on her side. She looked at Kelly as if she wanted to say something else, then pursed her lips and fought it back.

"Not soon enough, Karen. I have the rest of ninth grade and then all of high school to get through. And you heard him at Thanksgiving dinner. By then, maybe he'll think paying for his other two daughters to go to college is a total waste of money and he'll refuse. I won't be out then." Kelly sighed.

Karen sat up on the side of the bed. "By then, I'll have my teaching certificate and I'll have a job. You can come live with me. We'll find a way to get you a degree." She meant it. We could tell.

"Thanks, sis. That's nice of you to say."

Karen clearly couldn't hold it in any more. "Kelly, you do know Dad's cheating on Mom, don't you?"

"What? No. Who with?" Kelly acted shocked, but I knew she had told me that she thought the same thing for a couple of years now. The difference was she had always laughed it off before. "Who would want him?" she had always said to me and I always replied, "No one we respect."

"I don't know," Karen replied. "Whoever she is…" She paused. "You know, I want to hate her, but I can't. She isn't the reason he's an asshole to us. He just is. And he's probably just as much of an asshole to her as he is to Mom and to us." The room fell silent.

A horn sounded from the driveway. One of Karen's friends had come to pick her up. Big surprise, but she wasn't planning on spending Saturday night home with the family. "I have to run." She got to her feet, then crouched down next to Kelly. "Little sister, listen to me. Don't fall for boys who aren't good to you. Don't let them call you. Don't have sex with them. Don't even give them the time of day. Got it?" She kissed Kelly on the forehead and got up.

"Yeah, sure. Got it." Kelly watched Karen walk to the bedroom door. "Just one thing…?"

Karen turned as she opened the door. "What?"

"Are guys in high school better than the ones in junior high? Are the ones in college better than the ones in high school? Do they *ever* get better?" Kelly was serious.

"Actually, the ones in high school are worse than the ones in junior high. Then, in college, they slowly mature and get almost bearable. Sorry. I wish I could tell you something different. I gotta run. See you tonight, if you're still awake. OK?"

"OK. Have a good time." Kelly said to the closing bedroom door. She looked at me and then looked at her nails again.

"Sounds to me like we picked a stupid time to not be lesbians," I joked.

"Maybe we could just sleep until we're 21 or something. The next few years sound like hell."

"Maybe. I do think that Karen has depressed us enough that now we're going to have to do our toenails, too. Would you be ever so nice and go fetch us some chips? Just be sure to steer clear of the adulterer."

"If only I could," Kelly sighed.

CHAPTER 18

The next couple of weeks were tough ones for Kelly. She was angry at her father for all the obvious reasons. She was mad at her mother for not having any backbone. She was mad at Karen for no longer being at home *and* for telling her about their father's affair. And, in general, she was mad at every male human being, local or distant, alive or dead. It wasn't just her father who never failed to let her down. It was every junior high school boy and junior high school male teacher. It was the principal, vice principal, and janitor. She was mad at high school boys she didn't know yet and college boys she would never know. She was mad at the funny boys on TV and the handsome men in magazines. They were all a disappointment. All of them except for Wolf Boy. He had potential to not disappoint — or to at least not disappoint in the traditional male ways. He was different. Unfortunately for Kelly, she wouldn't be seeing Daniel again for several weeks.

Kelly and I had tried hard to not sit with Cynthia, Kim, Michelle, and the other girls in that group since the great lunchtime phallus-fest discussion of October. But on that Wednesday after Thanksgiving, there were no seats left in the cafeteria during first lunch. Kelly and I didn't have any choice except to sit with Cynthia and her friends. We walked over, asked if there was room at the table, and sat down.

At first, nothing happened that was out of the ordinary. Everyone was eating their cafeteria meatloaf or their American cheese sandwiches from home. Kim and Michelle were discussing the Christmas shopping they had done last weekend and where they were going to shop the coming weekend. Lisa made sure everyone knew when the *Peanuts* Christmas special and the Grinch would be on television. There was only a little talk about classes or even boys. And Cynthia hadn't said a word. That made me nervous. I knew Kelly was on a hair-trigger. Maybe Cynthia did, too. What is there about poking a hornet's nest that's so irresistible even when you know it's stupid and potentially painful?

"So you two," Cynthia smiled at us. It wasn't very convincing. "Here it comes," I thought to myself. I shot Kelly a look and braced myself. "What have you been up to lately? No one ever sees you anymore." That was well done. On the surface, it meant nothing, but everyone at the table knew that Cynthia meant *something*. It's not as if Kelly and I ever hung out with Cynthia or any of her friends, at least not since elementary school. So what was she getting at? Where were we supposed to have been seen?

I tried to run interference, but I didn't really know what she was talking about. "Oh, you know. Family stuff, mostly. We don't see that much of each other either these days. I guess we got together to work on our social studies project a couple of weeks ago, but... no. Not much going on with us. Right, Kelly?" She forced a smile.

Cynthia was taking her time. "I was talking to Kenny a couple of weeks ago and Kenny said that he and Eric saw the two of you over by the highway. You know? Behind the houses? I didn't think anyone went back there except for the dirt bike boys and the high school pot heads."

"Well, that explains why Kenny is always there, doesn't it?" Kelly said. Her face was getting flushed. It was hard to tell whether she was just angry about Kenny being the world's biggest loudmouth or whether she was concerned that we might have been seen near the tunnel.

"Really, Kelly. I'm sure I don't mean anything. No need to get upset." Cynthia smiled at the other girls. "Besides, if you and Beth need private time away from everyone, I'm sure that's your business. But you can't blame the boys for talking if..."

I did try to stop her, but Kelly was already standing and pouring her carton of chocolate milk on Cynthia's head before I could get a hand on her arm or get up to get between them. Cynthia shrieked and leapt up from her chair. After that, everything exploded. The scene quickly degenerated into the two of them wrestling and pulling each other's hair. Of course, there was the usual immediate gaggle of cheering onlookers: boys yelling "Girl fight!" and girls cheering for the girl they thought their friends would want them to cheer for. Someone at a table at the far end of the cafeteria yelled "Food fight!" hopefully — but no one took them up on the offer. All of the fight onlookers were openly looking around, hoping that it would take long enough before teachers came to break it up that someone would get in a good kick or punch. Luckily, Mr. Martin and Mrs. Spooner were there in a hurry and both girls were sent to the office at once.

The way I heard it, Kelly didn't even pretend to be sorry in front of the vice principal (Mr. Kincaid, another male disappointment). When the vice principal called Kelly's father, it was the perfect end to an ugly day. Mr. Nash sent Mrs. Nash to pick Kelly up at school and to tell her that he was grounding her for the month. And no adult, either at school or at home, ever knew what the fight had been about.

Kelly didn't call me that night. I didn't want to call her house as I figured either her father would still be yelling at her or she was stuck in her room "thinking about what she had done" and not allowed on the phone. Either way, her not calling me meant that things were unpleasant at the Nash house and I should wait until it mostly blew over.

I saw Kelly before school the next day. She looked tired. She looked like someone tired from trying not to be angry or at least trying to not appear angry. That kind of effort takes a lot out of you. She had her hair pulled back, something she almost never did. She was wearing one bracelet instead of seven or more. She had on lip gloss, but she hadn't put on any eye make-up at all that morning. I approached her cautiously.

"Hey, Kels. You OK?" I touched her upper arm and smiled.

"Yeah, I guess so. My dad grounded me for the rest of December. I can't use the phone this week either. That's why I didn't call last night." She looked down the hallway as she spoke. The other kids were rushing off to their lockers before homeroom. The halls looked so much more crowded now that everyone was wearing winter coats.

"I figured that was it. How did you manage to not get suspended?"

She rolled her eyes. "It was close. I refused to apologize to that bitch Cynthia, so Mr. Kincaid was about to suspend me. But then I told him that I would pay to have Cynthia's stupid little Madonna jacket dry cleaned. And I also said that I would be willing to talk to my guidance counselor about my feelings. That got me out of it."

"Ooo, guidance counselor! They're sooo helpful. If it's Mrs. Kinney, she'll ask you if you're doing drugs. She thinks we're all doing drugs. And having oral sex. But mainly drugs." I laughed. "What happened with your dad? Were the veins in his neck bulging when he yelled at you?"

"He screamed and pounded the dining room table like a mad man. At some point, he blamed my mother for raising me wrong, which naturally she didn't bother disagreeing with. But of course — to my dad — me getting in trouble at school was all about how it made *him* look bad. He never once asked me about Cynthia or why I wanted to pour milk on her in the first place or even if I had gotten hurt during the fight. It went on for almost an hour." She paused, shook her head, and then looked at me seriously. "Look Beth. Forget all that. It's like, what-ever. I'll deal. But here's the thing that's making me crazy. I can't go see Wolf Boy with you this weekend. I won't be able to get out of my house at all for weeks. I just... what are we going to do? We can't not go!"

I knew what she meant. I had already thought of this and had been trying to come up with a way to reassure her. "Kelly, Daniel's been fine without us all these years. I'm sure he'll..." I didn't believe what I was saying and was grateful that Kelly quickly inter-rupted me.

"He'll think we don't care, that we've abandoned him! Beth, you're going to have to go without me. You just have to! You have to go see him at least once by yourself just so he knows we haven't forgotten about him!" Her eyes were wide. She meant it.

The homeroom bell rang. The thought of seeing Daniel by myself made me nervous for more reasons than I could list right then. "We'll talk about this later! Bye!" And we both took off in opposite direc-tions down the hall.

The thought of me having to sneak off to the woods and visit Daniel by myself that weekend dis-tracted me for the rest of the school day. I couldn't concentrate on anything anyone said to me. My mind was elsewhere and probably wearing Kelly's uncle's long underwear. I would open my notebooks after I got home that night and find that I had taken notes in classes I didn't even remember attending. So, looking back, it shouldn't be too surprising that I didn't notice Eric Fuller until he literally ran up and blocked my path on my way out of the school that afternoon.

"Beth! I've been following you and yelling at you for like three minutes!" Eric was standing there between me and my bus, so I guess I had to pay attention to him. Unlike Kelly, I didn't currently despise the entire male gender (minus one). But in light of everything that had happened with Cynthia and Kelly, Eric wasn't currently my favorite male human being. He was friends with Kenny and Kenny had been bad news for months now.

"Sorry, Eric. I didn't hear you. But I'm in a hurry. I don't want to miss my bus." That would have been enough to blow him off, but for some reason I decided to get into it. "Besides, shouldn't you be wherever Kenny is? Cynthia seems to always be telling absolutely everyone who'll listen how she heard this from Kenny and Eric and that from Kenny and Eric. She makes it sound like the two of you have your nose in everyone's business and just can't shut up." I knew that was probably unfair, but I also felt like I should be mad at Eric for Kelly.

"Um… that's kinda why I wanted to talk to you. I didn't…" His eyebrows were raised. He was wearing a puffy green vest jacket over a pair of overalls. He was four or five inches taller than I was. I had liked the shape of Eric's mouth since a fourth grade fieldtrip to a local dairy farm. Another time, another time.

"You didn't what, Eric?" I cleared my head. "Hang with Kenny? Yeah. You hang with Kenny all the time."

"No, Beth. That's not I was going to say. I just wanted to tell you — not Kelly — that I wasn't part of all that other stuff. Cynthia made Kenny tell her about what happened this summer with Kelly. And I guess he told her I was with him when we saw you and Kelly that time on the street. Kenny is kind of a doofus, I know. But I don't think he knew Cynthia was like that."

"Right. Well, she's *totally* like that." I stared at him for a second. Honestly, Eric was cute. If it weren't for the whole Kenny thing, I would have thought he was boyfriend material. As if. "Anything else? I have to get to my bus."

"About Kelly…" He knew this was risky. He looked down at the sidewalk and then back at me.

"What about Kelly?"

"Look, I know Kelly's your best friend and all. And I like her. I do. I mean, I like both of you. Maybe you more than her, but… um… Like I said, Kenny is a real doofus, around girls especially. But I believe him about Kelly. She's the one who kissed him. It was her idea to… well, all of it was her idea." He looked me in the eyes. He was telling the truth, at least the truth as he knew it.

"Whatever, Eric. I have to go." I sidestepped around him and walked away toward my bus. I knew Kelly better than anyone, so I knew he was probably right about what happened. She wasn't going to wait for someone else to make a first move. But so what? She was my best friend. And, unlike Cynthia, Kelly didn't go bragging to everyone when she acted on her curiosity about boys and boners.

Screw puberty anyway.

CHAPTER 19

I spoke with Kelly several more times that week, both before and after school. And each time we spoke, she was more and more adamant that I needed to go see Daniel that weekend. He had become very important to her. I didn't know why, but I suspected he represented the possibility to Kelly that not all men were assholes. Perhaps he was more of a project. To me, Daniel was a handsome mystery who deserved a little sunshine in his gloomy forest hideout. I wanted him to be all right. No one should be abandoned. I finally agreed to do what Kelly asked and go visit him for both of us.

However, that did not mean I wasn't nervous as a cat on espresso shots as I crouched down and walked through the tunnel beneath the on ramp that Saturday afternoon. Had anyone seen me going behind the houses carrying a McDonald's bag? Had anyone followed me or called Cynthia to report my strange activity? Had anyone walked through the trees after me and watched me take the boards off the tunnel entrance?

About midway through the tunnel, I stopped being nervous about where I'd been. I started getting nervous for what awaited me at the other end of the tunnel. This is the part that had kept me awake the night before. I was still two months shy of my fifteenth birthday and here I was, going to meet a semi-wild, mostly strange young man in the woods. There would be no telephone, no way for anyone to hear me if I screamed for help. Isn't this exactly the sort of danger a young woman isn't supposed to go out looking for? On the one hand, I trusted Daniel. On the other hand, why did I trust Daniel? I didn't know him! How could I know him? He didn't talk. This was insane.

I took a deep breath, then another, trying to slow down my racing heartbeat. I would be fine. The world isn't the scary place of television cop shows and the network news. People go out and live their lives every day and all they see are the usual normal things. They live their normal lives. My normal life is that I've met a wolf boy. His normal life is a shack in the woods and the occasional visit from girls bearing junk food. That's all there is to it. Normal.

The first snow of the season had been followed by a second snow and a third, so there was snow covering the clearing between the tunnel and the woods. So I made my way along the slope break to the other path Daniel had shown us. I looked back when I made it into the trees, but I didn't see any cars or trucks on the road above. I didn't see any movement anywhere except for a crow flying from one pine tree to another.

As I walked through the forest that afternoon, I realized that I hadn't ever walked through woods in the winter. Mostly, I had been on hikes in the spring and in the fall, occasionally summer. But I had never been out in the forest after the snows began. So I was interested to see how the snow was scattered along the forest floor. Clearly snow made it through the pine trees. It clung to the rocks. The places with the thickest piles of maple and oak leaves had the least snow. Overall, the forest floor was a mottled grey, brown, and white.

The snow on the path was disturbed, but there weren't any footprints. I was leaving footprints. I would have to remember to ask Daniel about that, whether it was OK. I wondered when he had been this way last. I wondered when the last time was that he snuck through the tunnel in the middle of the night and ran through town, taking what he needed. I wondered if he had ever been anywhere near my house or Kelly's.

I found Daniel at his shack on the far side of the rock pile. He was kneeling next to a board that he had placed between two logs. He looked sideways for a second, so I know he heard me coming, but he didn't look up. As I got closer, I could see that he had a pair of dead rabbits laid out on the board. In his hand was a large hunting knife. Maybe I didn't want to stay that long after all.

"Hi, Daniel. It's me. Beth." I walked over to him slowly, holding the McDonalds bag in front of my waist. Of all the things I could have been feeling, I realized I felt embarrassed. Why?

Daniel looked at me, then leaned sideways to look around and past me. He gave me a questioning look.

"Oh, right. Kelly couldn't come today. She got in trouble at school and her parents won't let her out of the house for a little while. She told me to tell you hello." Clearly he understood what I was saying. "Kelly and I thought you might like another Big Mac. So, here." I reached out the bag to him. He looked up at me and he half smiled. That is, it was almost a smile but it was tentative and unpracticed. And then it vanished. He took the bag and set it down next to his feet. I guessed that he wanted to deal with these rabbits while it was still light. He motioned for me to come closer. I wasn't scared of Daniel or his knife. I was more scared of the bleeding rabbits. But, even though I hesitated, I knelt down beside Daniel just the same. In for a penny, right?

Daniel was obviously well practiced at skinning rabbits. It was less bloody than I thought it would be. He made a quick slice through the fur and then just pulled the skin and fur back and off over the rabbit's feet. Then he pulled the remaining skin and fur back over the head before cutting the head off. He snapped the rabbit's feet bones or joints and then cut off the feet. He repeated the process with the other rabbit.

"Is that all there is to it?" I asked. He shook his head, "No." After he slit open the belly of the first rabbit and started to reach inside, I decided that I didn't need to look any more. I looked away, trying hard not to imagine what he was doing, trying not to picture the actions that went along with the sticky sounds I was hearing.

I heard Daniel get up. I looked down to see the cleaned rabbit meat, sitting on the board. The rabbit skins were still sitting next to the board. But Daniel had taken away the feet and the insides of the rabbits. I saw him dump them into a hole far from the cabin and fill the hole in with dirt. When he returned, he saw me staring at his bloody hands and quickly went to the stream to rinse them off.

I got up and picked up the McDonalds bag. Daniel came over and picked up the rabbit meat and fur. Together, we went into the shack. Daniel shut the door behind us.

We both sat at his table as I watched him eat his hamburger. I assumed he would cook the rabbit meat somehow so that he could eat it tomorrow or the next day. For now though, he was happily eating his cold Big Mac and cold French fries. I tried to tell him more about Kelly's fight with Cynthia, but the words sounded stupid. Why would he care? If he cared about anything, it's that Kelly wasn't there.

In the end, I decided to tell Daniel about my father. He sat there, listening. I assume he understood most of what I said. I couldn't know whether he knew about the Vietnam War or even war in general. He knew what it was to die. I was guessing he knew what it meant to lose someone important to you, someone you cared about. Losing someone without ever seeing them? Even I didn't understand that one.

The light coming through the shack windows was starting to look bluish when I thought to look outside again. "It's getting late. I should go." Daniel and I both got up from the table at the same time. "I'll try to come back next week. If I don't or if I can't, Kelly and I will both try to get here the week after. I think she should be ungrounded by then." I smiled at him and then turned toward the door.

I turned back. "Would you mind if I gave you a hug?" I asked him. He looked at me and slowly nodded his head. I walked over and put my arms around him, just for a minute. I believe he held his breath. Then he exhaled and breathed in, taking in the smell of my hair and of civilization and of girl. And then the moment was over. I felt him try to back away and I let him go.

"Bye, Daniel. Enjoy your rabbits." I smiled and gave him a little wave as I opened the door and walked back out into the cold December air.

"Wait. You hugged Wolf Boy? And he let you?" I got Kelly on the phone as soon as I made it back to my house and gave her the full report. "You slut!"

"It wasn't like that, Kels, so shut up." I was pretty sure she was kidding, but you never knew with her. I thought my visit with Daniel had gone fine and the hug seemed like the right thing to do at the time. I didn't want her making me feel funnier about it than I already did. I didn't mention the part about him smelling my hair. "Kelly, Daniel was definitely looking for *you* when I got there. I had to explain to him why you weren't with me, why it was just me. I'm not sure he understood what being grounded is. I tried to explain. But anyway, he missed you and I told him we would be back soon."

Kelly laughed. "Yeah, well… he'll have to miss me for at least another week."

"Not longer? Why?"

"I'm hoping that my parents will drop this whole grounding thing in a few days," Kelly said. "It's my birthday next week and it would totally suck to be grounded for my birthday."

"Oh, right. Birthday. I always forget your birthday is so close to Christmas." I was lying. I hadn't forgotten her birthday. I had bought her a few new strands of twist beads at the mall when I was Christmas shopping with my mother. Kelly and I never had much available cash and we were already spending some of that to take food to Daniel. Small gifts were fine by us. "What did you ask for?" I asked her.

"I asked for some new boots. But what I would really like is for Wolf Boy to skin Cynthia like a rabbit, preferably on stage at the school's spring talent show. I don't suppose that's a realistic request though." She laughed.

"No, not likely. I'm sure she's all gristle and bone anyway. And besides, I think Daniel knows better than to eat animals that have rabies." I barely got the last word out before starting to laugh. I was sure Cynthia's large, furry ears were burning.

CHAPTER 20

Kelly was right, of course. Her father rescinded her grounding as soon as her birthday rolled around. If one were a more cynical person, she might think Mr. Nash only did that so Kelly could be seen out celebrating her birthday with her family at the recently opened, chain Mexican restaurant, where there just happened to be a photographer who just happened to submit the photo she took to the local newspaper where it ran with the caption "Local car dealer Nash celebrates daughter's quinceanara." And if the same cynical person just so happened to be Kelly herself, she would know for a fact that her father hadn't bought her that white dress with his own money because Gary Nash could never manage to keep anything secret, not his affair and certainly not a great trade of three free oil changes and a seasonal tire rotation for one crappy white dress. That Kelly didn't purposely pour mild salsa on it and pretend she had been stabbed in front of the photographer was a sign that she was simply enjoying the day for what it was. She was one year older and one year closer to leaving home. Don't rock the boat; pass the tortilla chips; and smile pretty for the camera.

And so Kelly and I were able to visit Daniel the next Sunday, which was the weekend before Christmas. She and I debated for several days whether or not to take Daniel a tiny decorated Christmas tree.

"You know, Kels. He may not even be Christian. So maybe he won't even understand or care about Christmas." I thought I should at least bring up the possibility. Besides, not knowing anything about Daniel's past made it a mine field of potential conflicts. Maybe he and that other person left home on Christmas. Or his mom died on Christmas. Or…

"I'm not suggesting that we take him a manger scene," she replied. "A Christmas tree is just a generic American winter holiday version of a tree. What's not to like? Wolf Boy has to like trees; he's hiding in them." In the end we decided that, since he did not have electricity, a tree without little twinkle lights wouldn't be as much fun. Plus a tree — even a tiny tree — would have been hard to carry through the tunnel and then through the woods.

Instead, we took Daniel a paper plate of colorful sugar cookies and one present to unwrap — a cobalt blue Bic disposable cigarette lighter. Kelly and I sat at his table while Daniel sat on his bed and unwrapped the lighter. At first, he couldn't figure out how to get it to light. But then Kelly got up, walked over, and reached out her hand for the lighter. He looked up at her and handed it to her. She kneeled down in front of him and, watching his face, flicked the lighter into flame. Daniel smiled an actual smile. Kelly looked back at me and giggled. When we left him that afternoon, Daniel let both of us give him a hug.

School was winding down to the two week holiday break. The "winter" band concert, featuring a multi-ethnic, multi-denominational set of songs, had sold out due to this year's introduction of a humongous tree made up of senior girls ringing hand bells and wearing reindeer costumes. When in doubt about ticket sales, increase the cast size. Everyone has relatives. Well, most people anyway.

The last day of school before the winter break was always only half a day. And nothing of any consequence ever got done. If a teacher could get a projector, she showed a movie. Any movie. Sometimes the teacher would simply say, "You can spend the period talking amongst yourselves. Just be quiet and let's not disturb the class next door. They might be working." As if. Closer to dismissal time, sometimes teachers would let students bring in food and the period was spent having an unofficial party. This year, the last half day of school before break fell on a Monday. It was the only day of school that week; it was a half day; and no teacher actually assigned work. The local school board must have been so proud, scamming the Commonwealth of Pennsylvania out of that day's student funding.

I was in my English class, less than an hour before dismissal, and we were having one of the unofficial parties. We had Coke. We had cookies. We had three bags of Hershey kisses. And someone had hung some mistletoe over the blackboard as a joke. Officially, it wasn't a Christmas party. But someone had brought in a Walkman and a cassette of Mannheim Steamroller's Christmas album. And Becky Krieger had drawn a Santa on the blackboard. It was hard to mistake this for some other holiday.

"Hey, Beth. You want some Bugles?" It was Eric. He was standing there, offering me corn chips that I could wear on my fingers like hats. You have to like a boy like that. You might even forgive him for the company he keeps.

"Sure, thanks." We both leaned against the wall, standing next to each other, not saying a word... chewing. We stood there listening to the music until the bell rang.

Christmas was not my mother's best time of year. She went through all the motions of the holiday, but without any of the holiday cheer. We always decorated our house the weekend after Thanksgiving. We wrapped the lamppost out in front of the house with multicolored lights. Each year we bought a fresh blue fir tree for the living room. We would spend a whole afternoon decking it out with twinkling lights and tinsel and ornaments we had bought each year, starting when I was only a toddler. All the presents were bought and perfectly wrapped before December was half over. My mom still faithfully sent out over a hundred Christmas cards each year, most with handwritten notes inside. The cards we received were carefully taped at an angle to the fireplace mantel as they came in. She baked cookies for family parties and for work parties and for the parties of friends from her own days in high school. She was dutiful in her celebration, right down to the last cup of egg nog with each set of my grandparents on Christmas Day, one after the other at their separate houses.

And yet, these were always the weeks each year when I was reminded that my mother's life hadn't turned out the way she had planned. The worst of it would start a few days before Christmas and last until New Year's Day. I would come out of my room at night to use the phone in the kitchen or to get a snack and I would find her, sitting in the recliner, blankly watching Christmas specials. She always had a tumbler of ice cubes and bourbon in one hand and the cable control box in the other.

"Hi, Mom. What are you watching?" I sat down on the couch.

"What? Oh… something with Fraggles." She took a sip of her drink and smiled at me before looking back at the screen.

"Are you OK? Are you hungry? Would you like me to bring you something from the kitchen?" I felt bad because she felt bad. I knew it wasn't my fault. But it still felt bad.

"No, honey. I'm fine. Did you get something to eat? I think I brought home some brownies from the office party. They're in a tin on the kitchen counter." She didn't look up. The Fraggles were discussing a Festival of the Bells. Someone in this story would be learning an important lesson about the true meaning of the holiday. It was almost the standard moral. Scrooge, the Grinch, Charlie Brown. It was more or less the same each and every time.

"Yeah, Mom. I'm good. I'm going to go read for a while before bed." I got up and kissed the top of her head as I passed by.

"Beth?"

"Yeah, Mom?" I turned back, standing in the hallway.

"I love you."

"I love you too, Mom. Goodnight." It was the most depressing "I love you" I'd ever heard. On the night she watched *It's a Wonderful Life*, I wouldn't even come out of my room.

CHAPTER 21

The week between Christmas and New Year's seemed to both drag on and fly by in equal measures. When I was home, there was nothing for me to do except read, watch television with my depressed mother, and talk on the phone with Kelly. On the afternoons when I was able to get together with Kelly, the time flew by and we both complained to anyone who would listen that obviously this school vacation should be extended at least until Epiphany and the end of the twelve days of Christmas, since that was what was in the song after all. It wasn't David Bowie singing *Little Drummer Boy*, but it was a classic just the same. An extended vacation would have meant not going back to school until Monday, January 6 instead of Thursday, January 2. And that would have meant another whole weekend out of school, which was never a bad thing at any time of year. Kelly and I existed in a "live for today" world in which snow-storms didn't exist and there were never snow days to make up at the end of the school year.

At first, neither Kelly nor I had plans for New Year's Eve. It became a joke where we tried to imagine ourselves out-lonelying the other person. But a couple of days after Christmas, things changed.

My mother's mood suddenly brightened. She told me over breakfast that she had decided to "go out with friends" on New Year's Eve and that she hoped I wouldn't mind too much staying home by myself. "Just lock the door and watch TV. I'll get you whatever junk food you want. I'll bake you some chocolate chip cookies, OK?" I was happy to see her happy and quickly agreed. But it was all I could do to keep my mouth shut. I was thinking, "That's great, Mom. Oh, and maybe your friends should try harder to give you hickeys in less noticeable places this time." But good for my mother. Maybe her sad season would be over.

"Really?" I had called Kelly and told her about my mother's plans, thinking I had just won the Lonely Prize. But Kelly sounded excited. "No, you are totally *not* staying home alone on New Year's. You're coming over here."

I paused a second before replying. "Nothing personal, but I don't want to spend New Year's with your parents. Not even in the same house. I'd rather sit here by myself and eat cookies 'til I barf." And I meant it. There was no way I wanted to start 1986 with Gary Nash and his smarmy comments anywhere near me.

"No, no! That's why this is so perfect! My parents are going out to some big party with a band and champagne and stuff. And they asked me to babysit Jenny. You totally have to come over and spend the night! It'll be great! I'll get my mom to take me to the video store to get some movies to watch."

I had to admit, that sounded a lot better than sitting home by myself. "You'll get something for us to watch with Jenny and then something for us to watch after she goes to bed, right?" I knew how babysitting was supposed to work. Jenny was too old for cartoons, but still too young for Tom Cruise.

"For sure. And you can bring all the junk food your mom promised!"

"What happened to Karen? Isn't she still home?" I knew Karen had gotten home from college on Christmas Eve. I assumed she would be home at least until mid-January.

"No, Karen bolted the day after Christmas. She went to visit friends in Philadelphia. She said she would just go back to school from there. I don't blame her. She and Dad started fighting as soon as she got here." She paused. "So, we're on, right? You, me, little sister, videos, munchies?"

I smiled. "I'll tell my mom." I didn't say it out loud, but I was glad I wasn't going to be home alone on New Year's Eve. When we were much, much younger — maybe even younger than Jenny — Joy Wyatt had told me that whatever you're doing at midnight on New Year's is what you're destined to be doing the rest of the year. That's why people kiss at midnight. I wasn't going to be kissing anyone at midnight this New Year's Eve, but I wasn't going to be by myself either. I could be spending 1986 having a good time with my best friend. I could do a lot worse, right?

CHAPTER 22

My mom dropped me, a sleeping bag, and an over-flowing plate of home-baked chocolate chip cookies off at Kelly's house at about eight o'clock on New Year's Eve. She was on her way "to meet her friends." It was 20 degrees outside and she was driving the car in open-toed sandals because she couldn't drive in the high heels she was wearing with her dress that night. I had complimented her outfit before we left the house. It may have been somewhat impractical at this particular moment, but she absolutely looked ready to party. She might have had a pre-arranged date that night and wouldn't see her old girlfriends at all. Or maybe her plan was to get drunk with her old girlfriends and for them to try to pick up men. I didn't know and didn't need to know. I just knew those heels and the cleavage in that dress weren't intended for Brenda and Betty. Not that I begrudged her for whatever she had in mind, either way. Life and Indochina hadn't done my mother any favors.

I gave her a kiss on the cheek, being careful not to smudge her makeup. "Happy New Years, Mom. Have a good time!"

"Oh, Beth. It's just me and the girls. I'll probably be home and knitting in front of the TV before midnight. You young folks have fun. Don't get sick on all that junk food."

"OK, Mom. I'll see you tomorrow." I closed the car door behind me and watched as she drove away.

Unfortunately, the Nashes weren't leaving for their party until eight thirty and Mr. Nash answered the doorbell. "Well, hello there, stranger! That's quite a plate of cookies you have there. Say, if you girls eat all those tonight, my wife will have to cut you out of your sleeping bags tomorrow morning. You'll be like three little sausages! Jaws of Life!" He laughed and ushered me in. "Kelly!" he yelled up the stairs. "Beth's here. Jenny, where are you? Come say goodbye to me and your mother. Sandy! Are you about ready? We don't want to be late for the passed appetizers. There's a bacon-wrapped scallop out there with my Gary Nash's on it!"

I stood there through all of this, smiling politely, my sleeping bag at my feet, and still holding the plate of cookies. Kelly galloped down the stairs, gave me a hug, and rolled her eyes when she knew her father wasn't looking. "They're leaving any minute now. I swear!" she whispered.

After Mr. and Mrs. Nash drove away, Kelly and I sat down with Jenny to discuss the night's big plans. Our first big team decision was to make a movie watching pit in the den. We made the pit out of couch pillows and blankets and sleeping bags. If we had been boys, we would have called it a "fort." Then again, if we were boys, there wouldn't have been a Cabbage Patch kid named Dwight and a Hello, Kitty pillow in the fort. And the fort would have smelled like boys.

We decided to have the food in courses along with the movies. Jenny agreed to not have any cola after ten, but Kelly and I decided that there wasn't any harm in letting her have a glass of Coke with the first movie, which was *The Muppets Take Manhattan*. None of us could ever figure out why the Muppets had gone to college in the first place, but the popcorn we made was both buttery and salty, so we just let it slide. The rats were funny.

The second movie we watched was *Splash*. I took the Saran Wrap off the cookies and Jenny helped Kelly make three giant bowls of chocolate ice cream with hot fudge sauce. We made it through the desserts, but not through the movie. At around 11:40, we gave up on Tom Hanks and the mermaid and turned on Dick Clark and his *New Year's Rockin' Eve* so that we could be sure to watch the big ball drop in Times Square. We turned it on just in time to see the "live" performance of "Shout" by Tears for Fears. Jenny rolled on the pillows laughing as Kelly and I made fun of everyone's hair, jewelry, makeup, dress, and shoes at the dance party. Naturally, we secretly wished we were there.

Kelly and I tucked Jenny into bed about a quarter past twelve and settled back into the movie pit with more soda and a bag of Ruffles. We started watching *Footloose*, but quickly decided that: 1) Kevin Bacon was funny looking; and 2) Kenny Loggins wasn't our kind of music. The dancing wasn't even that interesting. Luckily, Kelly had rented a fourth movie in case we needed a comedy. So we rewound *Footloose* and started watching *Monty Python's The Meaning of Life*. We were confused by the pirate accountants, but laughed hysterically over "Every Sperm is Sacred" and the sex education scene with the English headmaster quizzing his students on foreplay ("nibbling the earlobe, kneading the buttocks, and so on and so forth"). We were about to turn it off during the war bits, but then we came to the "Find the Fish" segment and our mouths dropped open. That was it for us; they couldn't possibly top that in our book. We hit Stop, rewound the tape, turned off the VCR and the television, got ourselves more Coke from the kitchen, and took the last of the cookies and chips up to Kelly's room.

"Oh, fishy, fishy, fishy fish!" I said, taking the stairs two at a time.

"And it went wherever I did go." That was Kelly, bringing up the rear.

We arranged our sleeping bags on the floor, side by side, next to Kelly's bed. Kelly turned on her stereo. We couldn't find any radio stations that were playing music we liked, so Kelly put in a cassette of Spandau Ballet's *True* and turned the volume down. Softly, we sang along to the first song…"Pleasures in the sand, warm within the hand she's holding."

"Did you hear that the school board voted to change our school over to a middle school next year?" I asked. It was a bit out of the blue. But then again, it wasn't. It was 1986 now. This was the year we started high school. "My mom told me. They voted last week."

"Wait. What do you mean?" Kelly sat up in her sleeping bag, facing me.

"Well, it won't be a grade 7, 8, 9 junior high school any more. It'll be a 6, 7, 8 middle school."

"What are they going to do with this year's eighth graders? Where does the ninth grade go?"

"They'll be coming to the high school with us next year. Ninth grade will be in the high school from now on. I mean, technically we're high school freshmen this year even though we aren't at the high school." I was half way in my sleeping bag, lying on my side with my head propped up.

"You're kidding me! Damn it. I don't want those twerps coming to the high school *with* us. Fuck." She pounded her pillow with her fist. "Well, that's just one more thing I'm not looking forward to about high school." She put pillow over her face and let out a muffled scream.

"Kelly! What do you mean not looking forward to high school? You and I have been waiting to be in high school for absolutely forever! We have big plans for high school!" Not that I had any idea what those big plans currently were because we changed them so often. For instance, we had recently discussed being crowned Co-Queens. Not of homecoming. Just queens. Like rulers.

"I've changed my mind. I just want it done already. You know? The thought of waiting three more years to get out of here just makes me feel like shit. I'm sooo done. I'm done with Cynthia and those other girls. I'm done with Kenny and the boys. I'm *totally* done with my parents. Now you tell me I'm going to get to high school and all the older kids are going to think I'm just like that bunch of eighth graders?" She was still slowly, gently punching the pillow in her lap.

"It won't be that bad. Maybe they'll keep the freshmen in their own wing of the high school and they'll have their own lunch period! But it doesn't matter. We'll be sophomores. We won't be the lowest form of high school life if freshmen are there, too!"

"And we'll have boyfriends?" Kelly attempted to smile but it came out crooked.

"Yes. Absolutely. We'll both have boyfriends." I had a moment of doubt, picturing the two of us, wide-eyed and six inches shorter than those leggy senior girls in their granny boots. "Maybe one of them will even be a junior with a car."

Kelly sighed. "I want all that over with, too." Kelly looked me in the eyes and I could tell she was serious about whatever this was that she was thinking. I started to think we should have just watched another movie.

"What?" I sat up.

"Having people talk about me behind my back. And first times. All those first times. Feeling like the clueless little idiot. Not being in control of what happens to me." She looked like she had a longer list, but stopped herself. "All that. I just want to get to the other side somehow."

"Yeah, OK. High school is a slog. But you muddle through it. Everyone does. It sucks for everybody, even the cool kids." I took a drink of my Coke. "I think it'll be fine. I honestly think I have very reasonable expectations for high school. Kissing is sophomore year. Whatever it is that my mother used to call heavy petting is junior year. And then, by the end of senior year, I'll have sex. That way, I clear the decks so that I'm not a virgin when I get to college."

"Well, I don't want to be a virgin when I *get* to high school. I'm done with that, too. Totally done."

"Oh, c'mon, Kels! You *just* turned 15. Who loses it at 15? That would be kinda skanky, don't you think? Besides, look at the gene pool you're swimming in at school. I know I don't want any of those heavy metal weirdoes coming anywhere near me with their sticky fingers and their stinky armpits." I thought of Eric and quickly blinked him away again. I'm not sure what kind of weirdo he was, but it wasn't heavy metal. This was all too serious, I thought. I should try to change the subject. "Hey, I wonder if my mom got laid tonight."

"I wonder if my parents bothered to kiss each other at midnight."

I thought about it a second before answering. "Probably. Don't you think they would kiss just because other people were doing it or because they thought other people would notice if they didn't?"

Kelly got up to change cassettes. "Do you think Wolf Boy has a hot bod?" she said, her back to me. I guess I hadn't been very successful changing topics.

"I think so. I mean, he needs a haircut and a bath, but… yeah."

"It's just…" She turned back around and flopped back down in her sleeping bag. "I know he was wearing layers and I was wearing layers and a coat and all, but when we hugged… he just seemed so… solid." She smiled, her eyes wide.

"He *should* be solid. Aside from the two of us trying to fatten him up, you have to figure he doesn't eat much. And he has to work out every day to get food and firewood. So, yeah. He's in good shape." I paused. "You know, if we're still visiting him this spring, maybe you'll get to see him taking his semi-annual bath in the stream. You would like that, wouldn't you, Kels?" I laughed and tossed a potato chip at her. "Ooo, Wolf Boy! What a hard, flat stomach you have!"

"Shut up, Beth. You're the one who gave him the boner." She scrunched up her face at me.

"Wait. *What?* I did not," I objected, even though I kind of knew what she was talking about.

"You hugged him first. I hugged him second. He was already hard when I hugged him. I could feel it pressing against my hip bone."

"That explains why you didn't want to let him go, I guess." She was right, of course. I noticed it after Kelly had stopped hugging Daniel and we were in the doorway, saying goodbye. "Got you a wild boy boner. Did you grind into it by accident?"

"Bitch. Bitchy bitchy bitchy bitch," she said, getting up to turn off the bedroom light. I chuckled and slipped into my sleeping bag.

I fluffed my pillow, waiting for Kelly to get back to her sleeping bag. Then I waited a minute more. "And I went wherever she did go," I said out loud into the dark room. We both burst out laughing and couldn't stop until we heard the Nashes' car in the driveway. It was nearly three in the morning. Gary and Sandy Nash got out of the car arguing.

"Night, Kels," I said.

"Night, Beth."

As I closed my eyes, I wondered what Daniel had been doing at midnight. And Eric. But mostly Daniel.

CHAPTER 23

It was nearing the end of January, the psychologically longest month of the year. The snows were coming two per week, one after the other. Snow plows left mountains of snow covering the sides of the streets all over town. You could trudge down the street on the shoveled sidewalks and not see the cars driving by, the snow piles were so tall.

Winter wears you down. Every bright blue sky day was separated by four or five days of gray, overcast skies. Mr. Witherow had told us last year that the days get longer after the solstice, which was forever ago, back in December when winter officially started. It didn't feel like the days were getting any longer. They were short and January dragged on and on.

Kelly and I hadn't been to visit Daniel for a couple of weeks. Every time I mentioned it, Kelly reminded me that we both had three long-term projects for school eating up our weekends. Besides, it was also much harder to get to the Daniel's woods now that there was so much snow. Even if our footprints were hidden on the forest side of the highway, we still had to make it through the field behind the houses on this side of the tunnel. It seemed too complicated, so we both agreed that we should wait to go again until there was at least a little bit of a thaw.

"There's always a few days of 50 degree weather around now." I said, sounding hopeful. "There was last year. We had that snowball fight, remember?"

"Yeah, I think you're right," Kelly replied. "I think there's usually a day or two of warmer temperatures around Groundhog Day." Living in Pennsylvania hadn't made either one of us a fan of Punxsutawney Phil. He had always been a fat, pampered, weather weasel to me. One or two warm days didn't make up for six more weeks of winter.

I hoped Daniel was OK. I realized that he had supplies and ways of trapping things to eat. And, even if Kelly and I didn't feel comfortable tromping through mounds of snow, Daniel would have had years of experience sneaking into town on winter nights just like these to find things he needed. He had wood for his stove, so he wouldn't be cold. I was certain he would be fine. I just missed him. We hadn't seen him since the weekend after New Year's.

I saw Kelly briefly on Groundhog Day. It was a Sunday and she came over to my house to work on her research paper for English. We both thought it would be a good idea if we double-checked each other's references, since neither of us had ever had to follow MLA style before. We could also proofread each other's papers.

But Kelly wasn't feeling well and didn't stay long. She looked pale and said her muscles hurt. It had been a bad month for flu at our school — in the whole country, I suppose — and we both hoped she wasn't coming down with that. My mother never let a year go by without us both getting the flu shot, so I hadn't even thought about coming down with it. But Kelly said that her parents only got flu shots themselves every three or four years. The only way she and Jenny got the vaccine was if they happened to be at the doctor for something else. And that hadn't happened this year. I quickly looked over her references for her and pointed out a few punctuation problems.

"Go home, Kels," I said, helping her put on her winter coat. "You'll feel better tomorrow. Nothing like a Monday morning in ninth grade gym to put a smile on your face and a bounce in your step." She groaned.

Sure enough, Kelly wasn't in gym that Monday morning. She didn't make it to school at all. I tried calling her when I got home, but Mrs. Nash said that she was sleeping. That didn't sound good. I told Mrs. Nash to tell Kelly that I hoped she felt better. I hung up the phone, hoping that this was just a 24-hour thing and that she would be in school on Tuesday. But she wasn't in school on Tuesday or Wednesday.

I got home from school Wednesday and heard the telephone ringing as soon as I opened the front door to the house. By the time I got inside and had closed and locked the door behind me, the phone had stopped ringing. I put my backpack down on the floor and removed my hat and mittens. As I was hanging up my coat in the hall closet, the phone began to ring again.

Chapter 23

"Hello?" I answered the phone and reached over to turn on the kitchen light. I was hungry, but didn't feel like making anything. Maybe there were apples in the refrigerator.

"Beth, it's me." It was Kelly and she sounded terrible. "I have the flu."

"Oh, no! I was wondering if that's what it was. You sound awful. Do you have a fever?" Everyone who had come back to school after having the flu kept talking about their fevers. There were probably three kids absent from every homeroom with the flu that week. On the bright side, Cynthia missed a whole week of school.

"I feel awful. I can't breathe. My head hurts. If I don't keep taking Tylenol, my temperature goes up."

"Do you need me to get you anything from school? Do you want me to get you some Starburst from the drugstore?"

"No, thanks. That's not why I'm calling." There was a pause and I couldn't tell whether she was coughing or crying or some combination of both. "Beth, I did something and you're going to be mad at me, but..." This time I could clearly hear that she was crying, then coughing.

"What is it? What happened?" On the one hand, I thought "How serious could it be?" On the other hand, she hadn't been anywhere near this upset when she had the fight with Cynthia. So there was lots of ceiling room there to be more serious.

"I've been going to see Wolf Boy without you and last time I was there I kissed him and now I have the flu and I'm scared to death that I may have given him the flu! He could get really sick. He's never been exposed to anything!" She cried more steadily.

"Wait. You did what? But you said we weren't going to see him until it got a little warmer? You said…" She was right. I was upset that she had been to see him without me. And that she had lied about it. "And you kissed him!"

"I know, Beth. I know! But… I did, OK? Be mad at me later. Just… I'm really worried that now he's got the flu. What if he's out there, alone and sick? He could die. Little kids die from flu. He could be like a little kid." She blew her nose.

I didn't know what to say. I was upset with her, but was starting to get worried, too. I just didn't want to let her off the hook so easily. This was wrong on so many levels.

"Beth, you have to go see if he's OK."

"Really? You expect me to go check on him?"

"Yes. Please go see if he's OK! I'm sorry, Beth. But, think about Daniel." I wondered for a second whether she had actually called him Daniel just then because that's what I called him. She never called him that. "If he's fine, then OK. But if he's not, you have to make sure he gets better."

"I hate you for lying to me, Kelly."

She started crying harder. "I know! I understand that! I'm sorry I didn't tell you or talk to you about it first. I just… I just did it and then there it was. I didn't think it through. But you have to go see if he's OK. Please?"

"Fine. I'll go on Saturday." I closed my eyes and shook my head. "What should I bring with me? I doubt that Daniel's ever stolen medicine. What have you been taking?"

"Tylenol for fever. That's the main thing. Maybe something for the stuffy nose. Water. Do you think you can take him some water? If he's sick, he might not be getting up enough to get to his water supply."

"Will he be able to eat? Should I take food?" It was the oddest feeling — being so mad at her and so worried about him, both at the same time.

"Keep it simple." She coughed. "Beth, I really appreciate this. I know this sucks. But…"

I cut her off. "I'll let you know what happens. Feel better." And I hung up the phone before she could apologize again. I didn't want to hear it.

By the time I went to bed that night, I had decided that I couldn't let this wait until Saturday. I would have to come up with some way to go check on Daniel the next day — Thursday — after school. I hated Kelly for lying to me. I hated Kelly for messing with Daniel's head and health this way. And I hated that it might get me in trouble the next day if I couldn't manage to get home from the woods before my mom got home from work. "If Daniel is healthy," I thought, "it shouldn't be a problem. The bus lets me off at 3:15. If I go straight there, I should be at the shack by quarter of four. I'll make it home by 5:00 without a problem. Of course, that's if he's well. If he's sick, that's something else entirely." I really hoped he wasn't sick.

I got up early the next morning and repacked my backpack. I took two of my larger textbooks out of my bag to make room for a flashlight and a half gallon jug of water. Then I went to the bathroom medicine chest and put a handful of Tylenol into a plastic sandwich bag. I didn't know what to take with me for congestion, so I took a half dozen pink Benadryl pills. I figured that, based on my experience, those would help him breathe and knock him out so that he could sleep. I didn't know what else to take with me. I saw a tin of Sucrets, but I don't even think my mother remembered how old those were. It might be better to have a sore throat than put on of those in his mouth.

The school day flew by. My mind was anywhere but where my body was. People talked to me, but I barely acknowledged it. I wasn't surprised that Kelly kissed Daniel. I think I was more surprised that he let her. Why? Why wouldn't he? Did I think there was a rule book for young, mute hermits that prohibited kissing girls that fall in their laps? Of course she kissed him. That is, of course they kissed. Still, given everything, she shouldn't have done it. Even without the flu, it kinda changed everything.

After school, I got off the bus at my usual stop and started walking briskly in the other direction. The only other kids at my stop were seventh grade girls and they were busy discussing Valentine's Day. They walked off without even noticing where I was walking and how quickly. I ducked down a driveway, into the field behind the houses, and followed in an existing set of footprints through the snow to the trees. Once I was there, I could make my way to the tunnel without any worries. My biggest worry was the fading sunlight. The sun was still up, but the light was getting yellower. "It'll get dark while I'm at the shack," I thought.

I wasn't surprised to find multiple sets of footprints on the far side of the tunnel, running between the tunnel and the woods. Even if Daniel hadn't snuck out to the town since the last snow, clearly Kelly had passed by here, coming and going to see

Daniel, at least a couple of times since we were last there. I wondered how many times she *had* been there without me in January. I frowned at the thought, lowered my head, and kept walking.

The wind was persistent and I was cold. Sunlight sparkled on ice-covered pine needles in the trees above. Somewhere in the distance I heard a car horn. But otherwise, the only sound was me walking across the snow-covered forest floor.

When I got to the shack, everything was quiet. Daniel wasn't outside and he didn't come to the door when I called his name. There wasn't smoke coming from the chimney, even though it was a cold day. I was getting more anxious with each step I took closer to the shack's door. Again I called Daniel's name with no answer. I knocked on the door. There was no answer, but I heard coughing inside.

"Daniel? It's Beth. I'm coming in," I announced, reaching for the latch. I opened the door, stepped inside, and closed the door behind me.

CHAPTER 24

Something wasn't right. I had been to Daniel's cabin several times in the late fall and winter. Daniel kept the stove burning nearly all the time, so the shack was always warm inside. Perhaps not as warm as my house or Kelly's house, but often warmer than it was at school most days. And Daniel had two oil lamps that stayed lit once the sun started going down, so it was never dark inside the way it was today. The shack was cold inside. The only light was whatever filtered through the window with its covering of brown cloth. It was so dark that I could barely see the table two feet in front of me.

"Daniel? Where are you? Are you OK?"

Again, the only answer was a cough. I couldn't see clearly, but I knew he must be over on his bed. I fumbled my way over and knelt down, feeling for him in the blankets. He was there. "Dammit!" I said to myself. I could feel him shivering with chills beneath the blankets. I found his cheek and touched it with my palm. He was burning up with fever and wet with sweat. "Oh, Daniel. You *are* sick. "

Quickly, I put down my backpack and got out the flashlight. I turned it on and used it to find the Bic lighter we had given Daniel for Christmas. I then used the lighter to light the two lamps. That would give me enough light to check the stove.

The room filled with a soft yellow light. I turned, scared to see Daniel's face. His eyes were half closed, but looking at me. He breathed through his mouth, though that seemed to be painful. He clutched the blankets to his chin, but clearly couldn't keep warm.

"You have what they call the flu or influenza. You caught it from Kelly. She's been sick with it this week, too. But nowhere near as sick as you seem to be. She sent me here to check on you." I walked over and stood next to the bed. "I have to say, you've looked better." As I said that, I noticed that Daniel's hair was shorter and more evenly cut than it was when I saw him last. Kelly. She couldn't resist that either.

My first priority was getting the shack warmed up to a reasonable temperature. "I need to get your stove going again." I looked around, but there didn't seem to be any firewood inside the shack. "I'll be back in a second." I went outside and brought a few pieces of wood back inside. I knew to use the ratty old pot holder to open the door to the stove. I chucked the wood inside and poked the coals with the nearby poker. They weren't dead. I blew lightly and the first signs of flame licked the sides of the lowest piece of wood. I closed the stove door and put back the pot holder and the poker.

"That should warm things up for now. I'll bring in some more wood before I go, but you *have* to find the energy to get up and put wood in the stove when the fire starts to go out. OK? You can't let the fire go out. You understand?" I knew he heard me and understood. I didn't need him to nod, but he did.

I walked back over to my backpack and took out the jug of water and the plastic bag of pills. I took them over to the bed and knelt down. "There's nothing I can do to make you well. You're going to be sick for a couple more days. But I can make you feel better. Do you know what pills are? They're medicine. These white ones are Tylenol. They will make your fever go down. Is your head hurting? Do your arms and legs hurt?" He nodded yes. "The Tylenol should help with that, too. So, first thing. I need you to swallow two of these Tylenol."

I got out two of the white pills. His hands were shaking so badly that I just had him open his mouth and put the Tylenol on his tongue. "OK, now drink the water and swallow those. Don't chew them." I tipped the jug to his lips and slowly poured water into his mouth as he drank. "You need to drink all of the water in this jug by this time tomorrow. You need to drink a lot of water to feel better. You've been sweating and... I think it just helps to get the bad stuff out of your system when you're sick if you drink a lot. Do you understand? But first, I think you should probably take one of these pink pills, too. These are Benadryl. They'll help with your breathing and cough. They'll also help you sleep, which is a good thing." Again, I put the pill on his tongue and helped him drink enough water to swallow. I put the jug of water down by the side of the bed.

I'm not sure why I didn't just go sit down at the table or pull a chair over by his bed. I could have sat there, waiting for the room to warm up, and then I could have left. But for some reason, I remembered how wet his skin had been when I touched his cheek before. I reached over and took the blanket out of his hands, pulling it halfway down his chest. I reached out and felt the cloth of his shirt. It was soaked through with sweat.

I was trying to be calm, but inside I felt anything but calm. He was really sick. He could die. If children and old people who live in town and have doctors can die from the flu, why couldn't a boy who lives in the woods? What kind of immune system could he possibly have if he didn't catch colds in daycare and in elementary school growing up? I couldn't leave him in those wet clothes. I knew that, too.

"Daniel, you're all wet. You can't stay in these clothes. You'll never warm up. Do you have other clothes you can change into?"

Daniel tried to prop himself up, but fell back onto the bed coughing. He was exhausted. Maybe the Benadryl was starting to kick in. He pointed to the back of the shack. "Are there clothes back there?" I asked. He nodded.

I had never gone back into the back part of Daniel's shack before — the part built back into the hillside. I was always there when he was and it would have been rude to just explore someone's home without them inviting you to. There was more to the shack than just the main room. There seemed to be a storage room of some sort off to the right. And then, just on the other side of a simple wall, there were these shelves. One shelf had a couple of crates and some towels. I grabbed a towel. Three of the shelves held clothing. I was able to find a pair of socks, corduroy pants, a t-shirt, and a flannel shirt. I bit my lip and also grabbed a pair of plain boxers. Damn you, Kelly Nash. Not cool. Not cool at all.

Something caught my eye on the bottom shelf. It looked like a Bible. I knew I shouldn't, but my curiosity got the better of me. I picked it up and opened the front over. It *was* a Bible. And on the inside was written the name *Whitmire*. I closed it and carefully put it back on the shelf where I had found it. I took the towel and fresh clothes back to Daniel's bedside.

"Let's start with the shirt." He nodded. He was still shaking too much to unbutton his shirt buttons. "Wait. Stop." I put my hand on his hands. "Let me just do this button and then we won't unbutton the others. We'll take it off over your head. OK?" Again, he nodded. He looked so pale and pathetic.

I unbuttoned the button and helped him take his arms out from under the blankets. I reached under the blanket and pulled on the shirt, making sure it wasn't tucked into his pants. As the shirt came free, my hand brushed the skin on his side. He was so clammy. This really did need doing.

He barely had the energy to turn, never mind sit up. So he lifted one shoulder, then the other, so that I could slip his arms through the sleeves. Because he was so sweaty and the shirt was already more than damp, it was a struggle just getting that much done. When I had his arms free, I worked the shirt up his back and in the front up as far as his shoulders.

"Do you think you can sit up just a little?"

He lifted his head and shoulders off the pillow. I wiggled the shirt off over his head and tossed it aside.

The cover was pulled back. Daniel was shivering. His skin sparkled with sweat. Kelly was right. He was lean, but muscular. Quickly, I rubbed down his stomach and arms with the towel, trying to dry them and maybe warm them a bit just with friction.

It was harder getting the fresh shirt back on. It wasn't buttoned, so I couldn't just slip it over his head. Maybe I should have thought to button it before trying to put it on him, but he looked so cold that I wasn't thinking. I had him roll sideways so that I could get his arms into the sleeves. Then I worked the shirt down his back and pulled the cloth around his sides to the front. I fumbled a bit, but I was able to button the shirt without much effort. The effort had all been Daniel's. He seemed more exhausted than ever and started coughing. I pulled the blanket up again. I suspected the blanket and the bed sheet were both damp as well, but I hadn't seen any extra bedding in the shelves in the back. This would have to do.

Daniel stopped coughing and looked at me. What was he thinking? I knew what he *should've* been thinking "These stupid girls made me sick. I should have kept throwing rocks at them." He should have. It's true.

"Do you think you can undo your pants for me? We need to get those off, too."

I think Daniel hoped as much as I did that he could manage that. He didn't ever wear a belt; I'd never seen him wearing one. So all he needed to do was undo the one button and unzip the zipper. He struggled for a bit under the blankets, then closed his eyes and sighed. He opened his eyes and looked at me. He nodded. Done.

"Great. That's great, Daniel. Now we'll try to do the rest of this as quickly as possible. OK?" He coughed again.

I pulled back the covers, exposing his legs from just above the knee to his feet. I was able to get his socks off without any trouble. Then Daniel was able to lift his butt off the mattress just enough for me to pull his pants down his legs and then off over his feet. I didn't have time to anticipate that getting his pants *off* wasn't going to be the hard part.

"Do you think you can get your underwear off or maybe just down some?"

I quietly prayed he would manage this. But no. He tried, but didn't have the energy to coordinate his arms, hands, and legs. He shook his head "No." I bit my lip and took a deep breath.

"OK. No problem. If you can lift yourself up again like you did before, I'll get them off." Right. No problem. I'm pantsing Wolf Boy and it's no problem.

I didn't dare move the blanket. I took a deep breath. Carefully, I reached under the blanket, up along the sides of his legs, found his damp boxers, grabbed a handful of cloth with each hand, and pulled on them as soon as he raised himself up. I slid the boxers — green plaid, nice — down past his knees and feet. I tossed them on the floor with the pants. I rubbed his legs down with the towel. They were muscular, hairy in a young man way.

"Almost done. Let's just work backwards and get these dry clothes on you." I picked up the clean, dry boxers and grimaced internally.

Daniel was looking more tired with each passing minute. He didn't seem to be shaking as much; the chills were fading as the Tylenol started to kick in.

But he also seemed to be fading on me. Maybe that was the Benadryl.

"I'm going to slide these up as far as I can and then when I say lift, you lift up and I'll try to get them the rest of the way." He sighed as if to say, "I don't have a choice in any of this, do I? Just do it."

I got the boxers up past his knees without much problem. I stopped in the middle to reposition the blanket. I did not want to come face-to-face with Daniel's... stuff... if I could avoid it. There's a time for curiosity and this wasn't it. I slid my hands to the side of his legs and grabbed the waistband.

"Ready? Lift!"

I shimmied the boxers up beneath the blanket. The middle got snagged, then let go. His eyes opened a bit wider.

"Oh," I said. "Oops. Sorry!"

I got the waistband of the boxers up to his hip-bones. That was good enough. "You can... put everything back where it should go, right?" One of his hands moved down beneath the blanket to his crotch, pulled or did something, and then stopped.

"So I guess you guys pull the waistband out some in front when you do that. Sorry."

He attempted a smile and closed his eyes. After that, getting the dry pants and socks on was routine. I finished and tucked in the blankets at the bottom of the bed. That would have to do.

I checked my watch. It was getting late. It was already dark outside. I would have to get through the woods and the tunnel and back to my neighborhood with the flashlight. My mother was going to get home before I did. I would be in trouble unless I came up with a good excuse. I hadn't even thought to leave a message on our answering machine. That was bad planning — a rookie mistake. I had to get moving. I took the flashlight and brought more firewood in from outside. Firewood is heavy. I made trips.

"Daniel? Daniel?" He looked like he was dozing off. "I know you want to sleep. I'm going to go. But can you open your eyes just a minute?" I didn't want to wake him up, but I was worried about what would happen after I left. He opened his eyes and licked his lips. They were dry. I gave him some more water.

"I know you're not going to feel like getting up. But listen to me. You *cannot* let the fire in the stove go out again. I've brought some more wood in for you. Just try to get up and throw another piece in the stove when you can. OK?" He nodded. I felt his forehead. "You should be able to get some sleep now. Your fever is down. But you have to promise me that you'll take more Tylenol when you wake up. Take two." I held up two fingers, even though I knew he knew what *two* meant. He wasn't a feral child; he wasn't a wolf boy. "And drink the rest of this water tonight. I'll either get back here tomorrow to check on you or Kelly will come if she's feeling better."

"But we won't come together," I thought to myself. "Because if I see her, I'm going to strangle her." I let that thought wash over me and then it was gone. I held Daniel's hand through the blanket and he looked at me through half-closed eyes. "Feel better."

I grabbed my backpack, turned on the flashlight, and left the shack for the cold walk home.

CHAPTER 25

When I got home, I decided to take the offensive and not give my mother enough time to ask me questions. I'd always been such a good girl that I'd never even had the opportunity to try this tactic, but I'd seen it work on TV dozens of times.

"Mom, I'm sooooo sorry" I said as I came in through the kitchen door. The flashlight was stowed away in my backpack. Aside from my wet pants legs, I looked like I always did after a day of school. "I meant to call and leave a message, but I totally forgot. You know Kelly has been out sick all week with the flu, right? So I went over to her house to deliver some of her school work so she doesn't have so much to do when she comes back. But I got there and I totally spaced on calling you." I made sure that I didn't leave any gaps in what I was saying for her to jump in. It's best to get the whole thing out there, all at once.

"You should have called. You know I worry. It's been dark for almost two hours." My mother was still in her work clothes, but had already started making our dinner.

"I know, I know. I forgot."

Just then, something else hit me. I needed to call Kelly before she called me. She was my excuse and it wouldn't do for her to call me first and get my mom on the phone.

"Darn it. Mom, I forgot to tell Kelly something. I need to call her. OK? I can set the table as soon as I'm done." I smiled.

I honestly would have felt bad about lying like this, but taking care of Daniel today was a good thing. This was one little bad thing compared with one big good thing. If someone keeps track, I'd win today on points.

I dialed the phone and waited for someone at the Nashes to answer. "Hello?" It was Kelly.

"Hi, Kels. It's me again." I wasn't sure how to work this with my mom still in the kitchen, but at least I knew she couldn't hear the other end of the conversation. "I forgot to ask you whether you understood that social studies assignment."

Kelly paused on the other end. "I was just going to call you. Did you go see him? Is he sick?"

"Yes, that's right. Both of those things."

"Dammit. I knew it. Thank you for going. Is he really sick?"

"Very. Will you be able to make it tomorrow?"

"No. My folks are still keeping me home from school another day. Wait... is your mom there?"

"Yes. That's right." I knew she would catch on eventually.

"Oh. Duh. So, no. I can't go tomorrow either. Can you go again? If he's that bad, someone has to go. And I really can't. My mom is here all day and there's no way I can get away."

I gritted my teeth a little. "OK. Yeah, I know you owe me big time. I gotta go help my mom with dinner, OK? Bye." And I hung up the phone.

The next day, I made it to Daniel's shack and back home without incident. I got out of my last class a few minutes early and asked to use the office phone to call my house. This time I left a message for my mother, saying I was stopping at Kelly's house again. That way, if I was late getting home, I wouldn't be making the same mistake as yesterday.

Daniel seemed better. I found him sitting up in his bed. The fire was still going and the room was comfortably warm. I probably hadn't brought in enough firewood to last a whole day — I know I didn't — but he clearly had found the energy to go outside and get more at some point. He looked more awake. He hadn't taken any more of the Benadryl, but he had taken several Tylenol. I brought more Tylenol with me, plus another jug of water and a couple of sandwiches I had made before school. I didn't stay long. I sat by his bed and talked about nothing important, just wanting him to hear a voice and know that he wasn't both sick and alone.

I left his shack while it was still a little light. The woods were darkening and the white snow was turning bluish as the sun went down. I got home before my mother and erased the message on the answering machine. Then I called Kelly to give her the report. She said she would be able to go see Daniel the next day. I told her to take him more water, food, and Tylenol... and to tell him hello from me. Kelly took care of him after that. I didn't go back — not with Kelly and not by myself. I didn't want to feel like a third wheel. Not with them.

I was coming out of the public library two Sundays later. I had finally decided to ask Ms. Dornan to help me look up the last name Whitmire in local news-papers. That was the name written in Daniel's Bible. It seemed reasonable that Whitmire was his family's name. And if that was true, maybe there would be some record in the newspaper of someone named Whitmire going missing. Ms. Dornan said she was happy to do it. She would look into it in her spare time and let me know if and when she found anything. I thanked her, stopped by the front desk to skim the fiction New Release shelf, and then walked outside to wait for my mother.

"Hi, Beth. Getting a book or doing research?" It was Eric. He was coming up the sidewalk, carrying three or four books to return. It was nice to see that he was a reader. That carried some positive weight with me.

"Hi, Eric. Just dropping off some books." He walked up and stood near me. It was cold and the fogs of our breath hung and mingled between us. I nodded at his books. "Anything good?"

"Just some old school science fiction," he answered. "I decided I wanted to read Isaac Asimov's original *Foundation* trilogy. You ever hear of it? It was really good. Reminded me of a lot of movies like *Star Wars*, except these were written back in the fifties, I think." He smiled. I suddenly thought of

Daniel's plaid boxers for some reason and started to blush.

"Don't you love when you find a book that you just *know* influenced something you like today, like another book or a movie?" I have no idea why I said that. It was borderline nonsensical, I thought. Dork.

"Oh, yeah. For sure. I hear *Star Wars* was actually based on old samurai stories." Eric probably could have gone on, but he stopped. "Do you…?"

"There's my mom. I gotta go. Do I what?"

"Nothing." He shook his head. "I'll see you in school tomorrow."

If he was going to ask me out or something, that moment just passed. "Yep. Good ol' school. I'll see you tomorrow!"

And I trotted down the sidewalk to my mother's waiting car. What is it about boys that makes them make everything about girls so complicated?

CHAPTER 26

February ticked away and things settled into a steady dull gray pattern of snow, gloom, and pop quizzes. Every break in the weather, every two days of above freezing temperatures, was immediately crushed by four days of bitter cold and ice or snow. March would surely come in like a lion riding a polar bear eating a Popsicle.

I forgave Kelly for lying to me about Daniel. I couldn't hold that kind of grudge. I would have had to consciously decide to not forgive her and I guess I never did. I didn't want our friendship to change. So, we talked every day before school and we sat together every day at lunch, just like before. I talked to her on the phone at night about mostly the same nonsense as always. And when I saw her on the weekends, it was clear we were still best friends. The one thing that I couldn't do was go with Kelly to see Daniel.

For her part, Kelly understood that she had stolen my half of our cookie. She had found him, but this Wolf Boy was always meant to be ours. I knew I shouldn't think of him that way. Daniel belonged to Daniel, not to us. Yet, I missed sharing this secret. He was supposed to be *our* secret, but he was Kelly's secret now. She only told me about him when I asked, which happened once a week or so. Yes, he had recovered from the flu. He was healthy again and seemed fine. He was busy digging himself a new latrine... and so on.

So it was a fragile peace, but one I was comfortable with. That's why I was so surprised when Kelly turned up at my house that Sunday afternoon, looking so serious. I felt boat rocking in the air.

"Beth, can we talk? I have to ask you for the biggest favor anyone's ever asked her best friend."

If that's what she said to me at the front door, before I even let her inside, then this was clearly going to be a whopper. The fact that she needed to pull out the phrase "best friend" right up front meant that it was going to be big. And then, as I thought about it, if this was going to be a bigger favor than Kelly asking me to go to Daniel's shack by myself, nurse him, and change his pants all because she had to kiss him, then she was right. This was going to be the Godzilla of favors — the biggest favor ever.

"Is this going to be about Daniel?" I asked as Kelly walked in the door and hung her coat on the rack. She nodded. "Let's go to my room." My mother was watching a 76ers basketball game in the living room. She looked up from her knitting and smiled at us as we went by.

I closed the bedroom door behind us. I flopped on my bed. Kelly sat down on my desk chair with her knees together, rocking slightly, forward and back.

"OK," I said. "What is it this time?"

I knew that came out sounding nasty even though I hadn't meant it to. Next to my mom, Kelly was the most important person in my life. I didn't want to be mad at her. I had worked very hard to get over being mad at her. So now it annoyed me that she might be about to say something that would make me mad all over again.

"I want to lose my virginity to Wolf Boy."

That again! Kelly and her agendas. I rolled my eyes and gave an exasperated sigh.

"Kelly, you know I don't think that's a good idea. You've only just turned 15. You're in some kind of hurry for probably all the wrong reasons. And we don't even know what Daniel's issues are. It's just a bad idea."

Wait a minute. I paused. That wasn't it, was it? That was an announcement, not a request for a favor.

"I know what you think, Beth. Believe me. I do. I've heard you saying those same things in my head every five minutes for the last week. And I don't want you to think I'm ignoring you. I always trust your opinion more than I trust my own. I mean, I actually agree with you about this. But…" Her eyes were getting teary. "But I'm going to do it anyway. You know that. I've decided. I want to have sex before I get to high school and there isn't a single other boy I know that I want to let get anywhere near me."

"And Daniel? Have you told him? He's OK with this? Does he even understand what you want from him?" I don't know what I thought. Daniel had been out in those woods alone long enough that he wouldn't have had anyone to sit him down and tell him about sex. But then, nature boinks. I imagined he'd seen bucks and does, rabbits, turtles. He knew the mechanics, maybe. And I guess I had never thought to ask — never wanted to ask — if Kelly and Daniel had been doing anything more than kissing.

"He does. I think he does. He understands enough that he'll do it when I ask him. It's just..." She was looking down at her hands as she spoke and playing with her bracelets. This was pure Kelly. She was getting very close to asking me what she came here to ask.

"Is this just because you know Daniel won't tell anyone? You're fed up with everyone talking about you behind your back, so you need to do this with the one boy who doesn't talk to anyone?" If she wasn't going to come out and ask me what she came here to ask me, I thought I might as well keep challenging her decision.

"No, that's not it! You know that. He's sweet. He's handsome and... I don't know... he's nice in a way other boys aren't."

"OK. Fine. Forget all of that for a minute. You're right. I do know you. You've decided and you're going to do whatever it is you're going to do. What do you want from me? This has nothing to do with me. I won't tell anybody. I won't try to stop you." Of course I wouldn't tell anyone. She knew that. But I couldn't think of anything else that would be such a big favor.

"I want you there with me when it happens." She said it very quickly and so quietly that I almost didn't hear her. Almost. But I heard.

"What? You've got to be kidding! No! No way!" This was like my third wheel problem elevated to *Nightmare on Elm Street* level. If I hadn't wanted to imagine Daniel kissing Kelly, there was no way I wanted to actually be present when they had sex. And for the first time. "Eww." I made a face.

"I know, Beth. I know. That's why I said it was the biggest favor ever. But I want you there with me. I need you there." She started crying for real. "If you care about me at all, if you're my best friend, you'll do this for me. You know I wouldn't ask something like this if it wasn't important. I'm going to do this, but I don't want to do it alone."

"What do you mean alone? You won't be alone. There's Daniel, remember?" I pointed to the Kleenex box on the desk. She took a tissue and blew her nose. "The way I understand it, sex isn't like going on a trampoline. You shouldn't need a spotter."

"Beth, please? This scares me."

"Good! It *should* scare you. Maybe being scared means you shouldn't do it. Duh."

"But I'm going to! It's happening! And it's happening with Wolf Boy! But I'm scared for both of us. I don't know why, but I am. Really scared. But if you're there, I know it will be OK. That's what I know for a fact. It'll be OK with you there. You're my best friend and you make every fucked up thing in my life OK." She smiled and then cried some more. "I need you there, Beth."

"You can't ask me to do this, Kelly. It's too much. It creeps me out." It did. And it didn't. I'd never even seen porn before, so I couldn't imagine seeing people having sex in photos or on film, never mind actually being in the same room. Interesting, but... ugh.

"Just did. Did it. Done." She wiped her eyes with a second tissue. "Beth, just think about it, OK? I understand that it's bizarre and that it's too much to ask and that I don't have any right. But hey. I'll do the same for you some time." We both laughed.

"Oh, yeah. Absolutely. When I lose my cherry to some high school boy, I'm gonna want you right there in the room, fanning us both with palm fronds and offering us chilled juice boxes." But in my head, I was thinking I'd never invite her. She didn't like Eric anyway. Everything was always about her and I didn't want Kelly to make a scene on my big day.

CHAPTER 27

"You're really not going to let this drop, are you?" A week had passed and Kelly was still trying to convince me to attend her deflowering.

"Not likely," she said, offering me the can of Pringles we were sharing. I took the last two chips and popped them both in my mouth at the same time. Two nestled Pringles is about the same as one fat potato chip, except for the part about Pringles being made from something two generations removed from an actual potato.

We were at the strip mall, sitting on a bench in front of Perkins Pets. The puppies in the window were napping. The temperature that day was in the 40s which, after the last couple of months, felt comfortably warm.

"I went to see Wolf Boy yesterday," Kelly said. "I told him that this was all going to happen next weekend. And I told him that you were coming along to be there with me."

"I suppose there's no point in my asking if he objected," I grumbled. It must be so nice for her. Mute boyfriends are so agreeable.

"He didn't say anything either way." She finished the last of her Pepsi and got up to throw her bottle and the Pringles can in the trash. "Does Saturday or Sunday work better for you?" She sat back down.

"Kelly, you know I haven't said yes." I looked out past the parking lot at the cars driving down Maple Street. The snow had melted enough in the first week of March that I could actually see over the snowbank and see the traffic. That was progress, at least. Spring would have to come eventually. "It might hurt, you know. What if you scream when he... you know... and it freaks him out? What if you bleed on his bed?"

"I won't scream. And I'm not going to bleed all over. I've been using tampons for three or four years now and they go up there without any problem."

"An erect penis is bigger than a tampon." I hoped that sounded more knowledgeable than snarky.

"I know, I know. I'm just saying that I don't think I have anything to pop or bleed. I suppose it could still hurt a bit, but I've heard that's only something that happens if you aren't ready." She paused and knocked her knee against mine. "And yes, it's definitely bigger than a tampon."

"Oh my god. You've seen it?" I suppose I wasn't really surprised.

"Yep. And..." She made a quick, stealthy up and down motion in her lap with her fist. "Cynthia Hale and Jeff Thompson can kiss my butt." I was going to have a struggle getting that image out of my head.

We were quiet for a moment while I tried to take all of that in. I was a bit jealous. Actually, since it was Daniel, I was more than a bit jealous. But I couldn't hold it against her (or Cynthia, for that matter). If I had access to a penis, I'd play with it, too. Just the thought of one inflating and deflating randomly (or — better yet — at my command) seemed endlessly fascinating.

"Seriously, Kelly," I turned on the bench so I could look her face. "I know your mother would never say yes to you going on the Pill. And you would die before you ever let her tell your dad. So, how are you planning to avoid having a little wolf baby?"

"I did research. My period was over last weekend. If what they say about cycles is true, I should be OK to go next weekend. But I'm not stupid. I'll get him to wear protection." She pointed to the Walgreens. "Since we're here, let's go buy some condoms. I can't count on him having stolen any of those, right?"

I groaned. "Kelly! How many times do I have to say this? This project of yours doesn't have to be a group thing. You could leave me out of it. Really."

"I could, but you know I won't," she said, grabbing my hands and pulling me up off the bench. "C'mon! Maybe we'll see someone we know! They'll see us buying boxes and boxes of condoms. There will be hushed talk about us all around town and it will become this huge scandal. Better yet, that might even give me something to discuss with the school guidance counselor." Kelly grabbed my hands and pulled me to my feet.

"Why do you think the people who run these drugstores put the 'family planning' products in the same aisle as the tampons and pads? Why not put spermicide and rubbers over with the diapers and baby formula? Doesn't that seem just as related? Maybe more so if you think of the if/then aspect of it. I mean, right? 'Use these condoms or else you'll be back here buying diapers in nine months.' Seems right to me."

We were standing in front of the Walgreens condom display. I didn't expect Kelly to answer. She was studying the condom boxes very carefully. I was only partly talking just to be talking. In truth, I was mildly offended that someone was proclaiming on a retail level that pregnancy prevention was a woman's responsibility, even when it came down to a balloon-thingee for a boy dick. Then again, maybe someone had done market research and knew that boys would never make a frivolous purchase of anything in the menstruation aisle. It had to be pretty serious business to venture into that territory.

"These all look the same to me," Kelly said, leaning over to get a closer look. She was right. To me, the display looked like a bunch of the same size boxes, but in different colors. Some boxes said Trojan. Some said LifeStyles. Some held three condoms, others six or twelve. "Did Ms. Walker ever say that reservoir tips were absolutely necessary?" Ms. Walker had been our sex ed teacher in 8th grade Health. She was also one of the Phys Ed teachers.

"Oh, my god. Ms. Walker was so useless! You could tell she didn't want to be teaching us sex ed. Even the banana she used for her condom demonstration looked like it knew. 'Just get it over with. Please!'" Kelly laughed. I looked around to see if anyone was looking at us. I noticed a woman behind the counter in the Pharmacy giving us the evil eye.

"I definitely want the lubricated ones. But I think spermicidal lubricant would be overkill. Sounds like putting Vicks VapoRub in my vagina." Kelly scrunched up her nose.

"You wouldn't think that if the condom breaks. Then you might want some spermicide. I mean, what if this so-called reservoir tip isn't a big enough reservoir? What if it...?" I made a motion with my hands demonstrating a balloon that inflates and then suddenly bursts. We started laughing way too loud for the Family Planning/Bleeding Women aisle of our local Walgreens.

"Girls, can I help you find anything?" A middle-aged woman in a white lab coat had come out from the Pharmacy. She wore a name tag identifying her as Phyllis Wing, Pharmacist. She wore a black skirt, black pantyhose, and black flats. Her arms weren't crossed, but she dressed like someone whose arms are always crossed internally. The fact that she clearly thought we were up to no good pissed me off.

"No, ma'am," I answered, trying to sound both innocent and sincere. I didn't feel either. "My friend and I were just confused because her father asked her to buy him a box of Extra Large condoms and we don't see any."

"Becky! That's not what he said!" Kelly piped in. "It wasn't the size Dad was being picky about. He wanted me to know that he and Mom really like the ones with ridges." I bit my lip to stifle a laugh. Before Phyllis Wing, Pharmacist could say anything else, Kelly quickly and decisively picked a blue LifeStyles box from the rack. We turned, burst out laughing, and made our way to the front of the store and the cashier. It was our only purchase. We were still full from the Pringles, so we didn't even buy a chocolate bar to split.

"Would you like a bag?" The middle-aged woman behind the counter handed Kelly her receipt and change. Phyllis Wing had followed us to the front of the store and was giving us a look we could feel on the backs of our heads.

"No. We'll use them here."

Kelly decided to walk me home before going home herself. Her father was being particularly nasty lately and any time Kelly could spend away from the house was time well spent. It also gave her more time to lobby me about next weekend.

"How 'bout this? Just go to the woods with me. We'll buy enough food for the three of us and we can all three eat lunch or dinner. You and Wolf Boy will get to visit with each other. And that will make everything seem cool again. You haven't seen each other in a while."

"You mean since that time you kissed Daniel, gave him an infectious disease that almost killed him, and you had to ask me to nurse him back to health for you? Since then, right?" I wanted to be clear about just why I hadn't seen Daniel in a while.

"Yes, you grouch. Since then." Kelly was tossing the box of condoms back and forth between her left and right hands as we walked.

"Oh, right. It'll be like old times, for sure."

Kelly decided to ignore my sarcasm and bully ahead. "So, you'll come with me and we'll all three have a nice time together, talking and eating. And then…"

"And then... what?" I interrupted. "I guess I pull up a chair and take out a bag of popcorn. Really? How do you picture... it working with me there?" I was making it sound funny, but I was also angry with her. Why was she being so dense about this? I couldn't understand why she wasn't getting how awkward this would be for me, even if —for whatever reason — it wasn't awkward for her.

"And then you can decide whether you need to leave or not. You can go outside and wait for me. Or you can leave and go home without me. Or maybe you'll decide it's OK to stay inside with us. Don't decide now! But just say you'll come with me. I want you there. You can come with me and then decide what you want to do once you're there."

"You do realize that if I go with you and then leave before, knowing what you're about to do, that would *still* be pretty weird, right?"

"Yes, I know. And I still want you to stay there with me, not leave. But baby steps. Come to the woods with me this Saturday. What if I can think of a way for us to take a large pizza? Wouldn't that be great? The three of us? Pizza and a floor show?" Kelly gave me a big goofy smile and nodded. "Awesome or what?"

"Shut up, Kels. Just shut up." I took the box of condoms out of her hand and stuffed it into her pants pocket.

CHAPTER 28

On Saturday, we each told our mothers that we were going to the other person's house to work on a term paper for English. Our parents never spoke to one another. This was even true when Kelly and I were younger and relied on our parents to coordinate times for us to get together and to drive us from place to place. Our parents barely spoke then; they didn't speak at all now. Unless something unexpected happened, this should be a story that would hold up.

We knew that, once we got into the trees on this side of the tunnel, we would be good for the entire afternoon. The only challenge was not being spotted or attracting too much attention on the way there. For instance, if one of our parents happened to see us at the strip mall buying a large pepperoni pizza to go, that might at minimum raise some questions about our junk food intake. So the riskiest part of the whole operation — at least the riskiest part not involving sperm — was meeting Kelly at Steve's Pizza Town and trying to get a large pizza into a backpack for transport to Wolf Boy's woods.

"I brought these sheets of wax paper. We'll separate the pizza slices with wax paper, stack them up, and then slip it all into my old backpack. You can put the Cokes in your bag." We were standing at a table at Steve's, fanning a take-out menu over the pizza, trying to cool it down enough to separate the slices. Kelly was dressed in her good acid-washed jeans and smelled like Jean Nate.

"Kelly, we didn't discuss this, but… I took some alcohol from one of my mom's bottles in the kitchen." I tried to keep my voice low. "I mean, I took some from several different bottles. They're all whiskey, so it's not like I mixed rum with wine or anything. She shouldn't notice. I just thought you might…" Neither of us had ever had more than a sip or two of wine or beer at family gatherings. I felt like such a delinquent.

"Good idea. We can mix it with the Cokes or something." She started stacking the pizza slices with the pieces of wax paper. She went over and asked the manager behind the counter for paper plates and napkins and a paper bag.

I packed up the Cokes and slung my backpack over my shoulder. On the one hand, I wasn't in a hurry. But if we didn't get moving soon, I might chicken out. And I had been too anxious to eat breakfast this morning. Now the smell of the pizza was making me hungry.

"You have the… drugstore items?" Kelly nodded and patted her jeans pocket. "OK, then. You ready?"

"Absolutely. Let's go!" Kelly put on her backpack, waved to the pizza guys, and we hurried off down the street.

Of course, the pizza was cold by the time we made our way through town, across the field, through the tunnel, into the woods, and all the way to Daniel's shack. It didn't matter. Who ever says *no* to cold pizza?

So the three of us sat down together at Daniel's table for a nonchalant, incredibly normal Saturday lunch. Kelly and I sat on the two chairs. Daniel pulled up a crate and stood it on its end to sit on. Yes, the conversation we had as we ate felt awkward and a little strange. Under the best of circumstances, Kelly and I had to carry the conversation when we were with Daniel, since he didn't talk. Under these particular circumstances, I was less talkative than usual. So it was up to Kelly to carry the conversation. To her credit, she was able to discuss classes, movies, politics, and her sister's taste in college boys for almost half an hour before she asked me if I still wanted to share the bottle I had brought from home. The elephant in the room was getting restless.

I didn't care for the taste of my mother's bourbon. I had one small gulp from the bottle before passing it to Kelly and quickly downed half a can of Coke to kill the burning in my mouth and throat. It made my stomach feel warm. The warmth rapidly spread to my face. I suppose I knew it coming in, but the bourbon seemed to emphasize that this was the most surreal Saturday of my life. I knew that if I closed my eyes for just ten seconds, I would open them again to find Daniel turned into a real wolf with green plaid fur. Kelly was telling Daniel stories about when she and I were in elementary school. We were cute kids and there were plenty of cute stories.

Perhaps I should have gone outside when Kelly looked at us both and smiled or when she got up, and pulled Daniel to his feet. I could have easily left right then. I could have found some big sticks and I could have used them to break apart some of the ice in the stream outside. Or I could have made snowballs and thrown them at one of the trees. Or perhaps I should have gone with my original gut reaction to this whole plan of Kelly's. I could have said my goodbyes, wished the two of them the best of luck, picked up my backpack, and simply gone home by myself. I could have even gone the long way home. That would have given me enough time to sober up before encountering my mother.

But I didn't do any those things. I sat at Daniel's table, my face burning from the alcohol and all that extra wood Daniel had put in the stove when we first arrived. The room was warmer than I'd ever felt it. I didn't leave.

At first I sat there, my hands folded on the simple wooden table, looking at the two of them over my shoulder. They stood near the bed, facing each other. Daniel's hands were on the sides of Kelly's arms. Her hands were on his chest. They kissed. I turned away and looked at the stove. I couldn't see flames anymore, but I could see the glow of the embers through the little window.

The embers eventually lost their fascination. When I turned back, Kelly was unbuttoning Daniel's shirt. I watched as she slid it off his shoulders. He was thin, but muscular. His stomach was flat and looked hard. His upper chest had patches of dark curly hair. Kelly untucked her top, gathered it near her ribs, and pulled it off over her head. Her bra was simple and powder blue. I knew her panties would match before she undid the snap on her jeans, slid them over her hips, let them drop to the floor, and stepped out. She reached up and took Daniel's head in her hands, pulling him closer. His hands slipped behind her back and hugged her close as they began kissing again. They were so different looking, I thought. He was dark to her light, tall to her short, quiet to... well, to Kelly.

Slowly, Kelly reached behind her back and un-hooked the clasp on her bra. She let the shoulder straps fall off her arms and tossed the bra aside. She took Daniel's hands in hers and placed them on her bare breasts. Again, I felt I had to look away. When I did, I saw the bottle with the last of the bourbon on the table just in front of me. I reached for it and drank it down, chasing it with the last of Kelly's Coke. That should do it.

I turned around in my chair to face them. They didn't seem to notice and that was fine by me. I pulled my feet up onto the chair and hugged my knees to my chest, laying my cheek on my arms so that I looked at them almost sideways. They were standing, but in my eyes they looked like they were already lying down. I heard a crow cawing outside and the crack and pop of wood burning in the stove. Kelly was talking to Daniel, but I couldn't hear what she said. For some reason, the sounds of their kisses traveled far more easily to my ears than the sounds of their words. Their kisses were a roar in my ears. Kisses and crows.

I loved how the two of them looked both natural and fumbling at the same time. I remembered what it looked like when two eighth graders had tried to slow dance with each other at last spring's Spring Fling dance. It was the same jumble of flowing and halting, lurching mixed with certainty. Kelly's hands on Daniel's arms seemed steady and sure. His hand on her face was also tender, steady and sure. But when Kelly went to touch Daniel's side or move her hand around to his back, it was like a stumble. Her hand moved one way, then the other, and then finally found what it was looking for, her fingers sliding around the far side of his ribs and pulling him close. And Daniel, like the boy not knowing how to dance, stood in one place, not wanting to move his hands from Kelly's breasts, afraid to either squeeze or let go, aware of the music but blinded by the barefoot girl on tip-toes.

The air inside the shack seemed to shimmer and buzz. I wondered if I was actually hearing them breathe. I could hear my own breathing. My one ear was pressed against my arm in that way that makes you think you can hear your breath coming through the sides of your head. My breathing was right there in my head, but I imagined that theirs was louder. They kissed. I sighed. The room quivered.

Kelly backed away from Daniel, looked down, and undid the button on his Levis. Slowly, she slid down the zipper. Then she opened the jeans waistband past his hipbones in the front and slid his pants down past his rear, down his thighs, letting them drop until they were bunched up around his lower legs. Daniel was wearing the same green plaid boxers I had taken off of him the day he was so sick. I smiled, even though that thought made me as sad as it did happy. He looked over at me just then, catching me in that thought, catching me looking at him in those boxers and smiling. I was suddenly embarrassed. His underwear was sticking out a lot more today than it had the last time.

Daniel tried to pull his feet out of the pants at his ankles, but he couldn't. Kelly let out a little laugh. "Wait, wait. I can help you." But first she stepped closer to Daniel and rubbed her belly against that bulge in his boxers. She giggled and got down on her knees at Daniel's feet. She slid each pants leg farther down toward Daniel's heels and then helped him step out. She shoved the pants toward the foot of the bed.

Kelly ran her hands up along the backs of Daniel's bare legs, down along the sides, then slowly up again along the fronts of his legs. Looking up at him, she hooked her fingers inside the back waistband of his boxers and pulled them down over his butt. They slid down at an angle along his sides, started moving down at the front — and then got caught on his erection in the front — before pulling it down enough to slide past it. Daniel's boner bounced several times when the boxers finally let it go. Kelly laughed. She reached up, lifted it a little with her thumb and forefinger, and then let it drop, just to see it bounce again.

As Kelly removed the underwear from Daniel's feet, I will admit I stared at his penis. Karen had given Kelly a copy of *Playgirl* last year, so I had seen pictures.. But I'd never seen one erect before, just the silly line drawings in our health textbook. Now Daniel's penis was standing straight out — no, maybe angled just a bit off the horizontal — and it was bobbing. I bet they don't mention that in any of the sex ed classes, even the good ones. Daniel was standing still but his dick was bobbing up and down with the beat of his heart. It had a pulse.

I closed my eyes. I didn't want either of them to see me staring. Not that they should blame me if I did. Screw 'em, I was invited. When I opened my eyes again, I saw Daniel was looking at me. I can't describe the look on his face. He didn't smile. But he didn't seem sad or embarrassed. He was the least embarrassed naked person who ever lived, standing there in his shack, one nearly naked girl fumbling around in her discarded pants pocket for a condom, another girl staring at him from across the room. I felt somehow that he knew more about being in this moment than either Kelly or I did. Life was a bunch of moments.

Kelly opened the condom wrapper and took out the condom. She turned it, looking at both sides so she could find which way it unrolled. When she looked up again, her forehead just missed Daniel's erection. Kelly leaned back a little. "Whoa. You should never look at one of these things straight on like that, all of a sudden." She used both hands to very carefully place the condom on Daniel's penis — which continued to move without any conscious help from him — and then slowly rolled the condom down over the head and then down over the shaft. She admired her work. "I guess this is the reservoir tip," she laughed, poking gently at a little floppy bit of latex at the end.

"Show time," she said, getting to her feet. She looked over at me and smiled, wiggling her panties off and tossing them aside. She gave me her traditional, wide-eyed, "here goes nothing" look, then took Daniel's arm and steered him to the bed. Kelly pulled back the covers, sat down, and stretched herself out on the mattress. Daniel sat down on the edge of the bed, just looking at her. Kelly took his hand and placed it, palm down, on her belly. He leaned over and kissed her again, then slipped into the bed beside her. She covered them both with the blanket.

I watched the blanket move in undulations, as if covering the slow, irregular movements of several horny pythons. I felt my face burning again and I closed my eyes. Again, I heard a crow outside and then my stomach gurgling. I took a deep breath. My ears refocused on the bed. There were renewed sounds of kissing, of the mattress pressing on the slats and the bed adjusting itself on the shack floor under their weight. I heard the blankets rustle and more kissing. I even thought I heard Daniel moan once. There was talking, more kissing, more movement. Then silence.

"Beth?" I opened my eyes. It was Kelly. She was reaching out her hand to me from the bed. Daniel's face hung above hers. His body, beneath the blanket, hung above hers.

I looked across the too-hot room at Kelly's face. Her face was filled with hope and love, her eyes wide with pleasure and with joy. There it was, I thought — a moment. It was the best moment Kelly had found in forever. Instead of turning away, instead of leaving her there, I let it all go — all of the overthinking and Sunday school sermons and my mother's dinnertime lectures and the countless television afterschool specials and movies with their "girl in trouble" storylines and the teen romance novels and the Victorian morality plays. To hell with all of that. Now mattered more than any of what came before. I stood up.

I picked up my chair and they both watched me as I walked it over to the side of the bed. I set the chair down. I caressed Daniel's face with the back of my fingers. Then I leaned over and kissed him on the mouth. His lips were warm.

Then I sat down in the chair facing Kelly's naked shoulders and her open-mouthed smile. For now, she was happy. Again, she reached her hand out to me. And I took it.

I took Kelly's hand and I held it as Daniel pushed inside her for the very first time and she gasped. (No, she didn't scream. There wasn't pain or blood or any of the rest of that cherry popping, oh-my-god, this is the scary thing that happens when you lose your virginity bullshit. Foreplay, people. And the movies lie.) I held her hand as her breasts began to rock back and forth and her cheeks turned pink. I held her hand, watching her look up at Daniel, then over at me, then at nothing — her eyes closing briefly, tightening her grip on my hand, pulling me into their rhythm. I held her hand, smiling at her when she pulled her knees back toward her chest beneath the blankets and arched her back. I held her hand when she licked her lips and looked at me with love, her eyes wide, trying to tell me what it was like with a wordless silence more powerful than any Wolf Boy's.

I was Kelly's best friend. I took her hand and I held it until they were done.

CHAPTER 29

I never did go back to Daniel's shack. As much as I felt that Daniel was my friend as well as Kelly's, and even though the weird afternoon at the cabin was both odd and special, my feelings about being a third wheel had gotten even worse since that day with the pizza and crows. It just felt impossible to go back there now, either with Kelly or without her. Not that Kelly asked me to go with her. She didn't mention Daniel at all when I saw her. I assumed she was still going to see him by herself. It wasn't any of my business what they did if and when they got together. When she and I talked before school or at lunch or on the phone at night, we went back to discussing whatever it was we talked about before she found Wolf Boy. It was fine. It had to be fine.

For my birthday, I got my mother to drop me and Kelly off at the General Cinemas 12-Plex so we could finally get to see *Pretty in Pink*. It had come out the last weekend in February, but we were too busy ravaging a feral boychild that weekend to go see it. My mom gave us money for the tickets and for popcorn and candy, so we were well stocked when we settled into our seats in the theater. It was a Saturday matinee and we got there a little early. We started nibbling as we watched the other people wander in and spread out in the mostly empty theater.

"Remember when the Mr. Kincaid sent me to the guidance counselor after I had the fight with Cynthia?" Kelly asked. She was saving her popcorn for the movie, but was already one third of the way through her box of Milk Duds.

"Yeah, but you never told me you actually went. Did you go? Was it Mrs. Kinney? You would have made her very happy if you told her you had sex, particularly if you made it sound lurid." I liked the word *lurid*. There were never enough conversations in which I could throw the word *lurid*. I stuck out my hand and Kelly handed me a Milk Dud.

"No, I didn't see Mrs. Kinney. I spoke with Mrs. Spradlin."

"I haven't heard anything about her. Doesn't she usually just talk to students about their grades and stuff like that?" I was distracted by two boys who walked in and sat down together. Why would guys our age come see *Pretty in Pink* if they weren't girls?

"I guess, but I was there because of my fight with Cynthia. Anyway, I'd seen her a few times since the fight. And I made the big mistake of thinking I could trust her. You know, like I thought there was the same sort of doctor patient privilege or something? But then I went into her office yesterday after school and my parents were there. She had totally called them — not the other way around — and asked them to come in so we could all discuss 'as a team' how unhappy I was at home."

"Let me guess. Your mom and dad came off looking like the world's most perfect parents and they made you look like the spoiled trouble child." I knew the Nashes well enough to picture the entire meeting in my mind, right down to Sandy Nash in her blouse with padded shoulders, her hands folded in her lap, and Gary Nash smiling that teeth-whitened, insincere smile of his.

"It was a disaster. Every awful thing that my father has ever said or done to me or to Jenny or to Karen, he either denied or made out as some misunderstanding. And my mom just sat there. She sat there, knowing the truth, but not saying a word. After ten minutes or so, I was so upset that I started yelling at her. Not at my dad. I was yelling at my mom! I begged her to talk, just to fucking open her mouth and back me up. But she didn't. She wouldn't even look at me. She just turned to Mrs. Spradlin and said that I'd always been such a headstrong girl. Then the three of them discussed getting me a professional counselor — a shrink, I guess — while I was still sitting there crying."

"Wow. That sounds worse than awful!"

"No, wait. Beth, it got *worse*. All the way home in the car, my father screamed at me about how I had ruined his afternoon, about how ungrateful I was, how stupid I was, what an embarrassment I was to him and to my mother. And she still didn't say a word. Nothing. I wanted to hurt her. I wanted to scream in her face that he was fucking some other woman. That he was the real embarrassment. But I didn't. What difference would it make? She wouldn't change. Things don't change."

The theater house lights dimmed. I looked over at Kelly and saw her wipe tears off her cheek. So far, being 15 didn't seem to have any noticeable advantages over being 14. We still had the same highs and lows. We were still at the mercy of parents and teachers, hormones and fate. The previews began and I handed Kelly the popcorn. For the next hour and a half, at least we had Blane and Duckie.

I saw less and less of Kelly as spring arrived. She was never available to meet up with me after school or on the weekends. At first I thought that maybe she was spending her time sneaking off to the woods to be with Daniel. But, as her mood got darker and angrier, I knew that wasn't what was happening at all. Finally, one day in early April, I was able to get her alone at lunch and ask her directly.

"What's going on with you? Is something going on at home that I don't know about? Like, worse than the usual? Or are you spending all of your time with Daniel?" I took a bite of my turkey sandwich. I didn't want to sound jealous and it worried me that it had come out of my mouth sounding that way. "I mean, it would OK if you were, but…"

"No, it's isn't Daniel. I haven't seen him at all for almost two weeks." She wasn't eating. She hadn't even opened her lunch bag.

"Then…home?" I put down my sandwich.

"Yeah. My parents are all over me. They told me to not even think about asking to leave the house except for school. It's worse than being grounded. I can't even call you. I come to school; I go home; I listen to my father yell at me and Jenny at dinner. Then I go to bed so I can have the same bullshit day tomorrow and the next day. That's it. That's my entire life right now." She paused. "I'm sorry. I know I'm not being much of a friend right now. I feel like I've bailed on both you and Daniel. I feel really bad about it. It sucks so bad, Beth."

"Kels, I'm sooo sorry. But it'll get better, right?" It hadn't so far. I knew that.

"I don't know. I don't think so. Everything seems so out of control right now. I have you and I have Daniel, but it's not like I can see either one of you. I can't talk to either one of you. I can't even get word to Daniel that he shouldn't worry about me or think I've abandoned him."

I knew I should have volunteered to go see Daniel for her and make her excuses, but I couldn't. That part was complicated for me and Kelly knew it. She didn't ask. We split my pack of gummies and hugged when the bell rang before rushing off to our afternoon classes.

Unfortunately, Kelly was right. Things were only getting more and more out of control. Early the next week, I was in gym when Kim told me that Kelly had been sent to the office last period. Kim said that Kelly had started cursing out Cynthia in the hallway between classes and then flipped off a Spanish teacher when she tried to separate them. Everyone was talking about it the rest of the school day. No one said anything to me, but I knew what the whispering was about. I was really worried about Kelly and wondered how I could talk to her to make sure she was OK.

I was in the kitchen at my house after school, making a salad for dinner before my mother got home. The phone rang. I quickly rinsed my hands and answered the phone on the fourth ring. "Hello?" I was surprised to hear Kelly's voice on the other end of the line.

"Beth, it's me. Don't talk. I have to be quick. I only have a couple of minutes before my mother gets back from picking up Jenny or before my dad gets here. Everything is totally fucked up. I got suspended because of that thing today with Cynthia. Then my mom came home from picking me up at school and decided to search my room for drugs. As if. She didn't find any drugs, but she did find the condoms in my dresser. And she called my dad at work and told him. He was furious and now he's coming home from work early to deal with me. Beth, why would my mom *do* that? Doesn't she know…?" And she started to cry. "Shit. He's home. I'll try to call you again, but…"

"Get off that phone, you little whore!" I heard a slam and then a click as someone hung up the phone.

My mother found me crying at the kitchen table next to the cutting board and some partly cut up bell pepper. I couldn't tell her what was wrong when she asked me. The best I could get out was one word:

"Everything."

CHAPTER 30

Kelly wasn't in school the next day. And while I was worried about her, everyone knew that she had been suspended for two days. So she wasn't supposed to return to school until Thursday at the earliest. I wanted to call her, but knew I would get one of her parents and they wouldn't let me speak to her. I didn't know what they thought about me. Maybe they thought I was a little whore, too. I knew what I thought of them.

But then Thursday came and went with no sign of Kelly. I looked for her before school on Friday and she was still nowhere to be found. Now people started asking me where she was. Our friends asked carefully. Cynthia's gaggle asked in a way that made it clear they hoped Kelly was dead in a ditch. Mostly, I shook my head to all comers. I didn't know much more than they did about where she was. And the things I did know more about, I wasn't about to discuss with any of them.

I walked slowly down my street after getting off the bus that afternoon, thinking about Kelly, about Daniel, and about me. I was miserable. Why was everything so screwed up? Not just lately, but in general? Why did my father get killed? If he was just going to get killed, why did he have to get my mom pregnant? Why was she still by herself after all these years? Why couldn't she just move on? Who took Daniel into the woods only to leave him there alone? What had Kelly done that had been so wrong? Why didn't anyone see what creeps her parents were?

I didn't have a single answer to a single question. Each wrong and inequity I could think of got piled on top of the last one and the one before that. Spring was turning out to be even more depressing than winter. The street sweepers used to make me so happy when I was a little girl because they took away the sand and gravel that made it so dangerous to ride a bike in early April. Now they just seemed loud and conspiratorial and they could never sweep away the stuff that was bothering me.

I was almost to my house when I looked up from my feet and the sidewalk and noticed a strange car in my driveway. The front passenger door opened and Kelly got out, closing the door behind her. I dropped my backpack in my front yard as I ran across the lawn to hug her.

"I've missed you so much. Are you OK?" I said into her hair. My cheek was pressed to her shoulder. I didn't want to let her go.

"Beth, I'm leaving town." Gently, she pushed me away so that she could look me in the eyes as she talked. "I called my aunt — my mother's sister — and she's willing to let me live with her until school ends. After that, Karen said I could live with her in off-campus housing at the university this summer."

"What? Kelly, you can't go! I'll never see you." I started to cry. "This is all so fucked up!"

"I know. I know. But I can't stay. I really can't." She looked down, blinked away her own tears, and looked back at me. The left side of her face was bruised. I hadn't noticed that before.

"Kelly! Did he hit you?" I tried to look at her more closely, but she turned that side of her face toward the car. Then she looked back down at the ground.

"Sort of, I guess. You were on the phone when he came in. You heard how mad he was. He grabbed me. I pulled away. And then I fell into the wall."

"I heard him call you a whore and then the line went dead."

"I have to say that wasn't the worst thing he called me. The yelling went on and on. I got so upset and so mad that I told him that I knew about his affair. And then he really did smack me. Same side of my face, naturally. My mother found me there on the floor when she finally came in." Kelly laughed weakly. "And you know what? She didn't even ask what had happened. All she said to me was how disappointed she was in me. In me."

I didn't know what to say. I didn't want to bring up Jenny to Kelly. I knew it must have been eating her up inside to know she was leaving Jenny there in that horrible house just the way Karen had left her two years ago. But what could she do about it? She was just 15.

And while I wanted to be selfish and tell her she couldn't abandon me or Daniel, I didn't have the right. What good would that have done? I didn't want to make her feel bad for doing the only thing she could see clearly to do. What she did with Daniel was something Kelly chose to do because she thought it would make her present and her future hurt less. This wasn't all that much different. I knew she had to take the shot.

"So can we call each other? Can I come see you some time? Where does your aunt live?" I was wiping tears on the sleeve of my jacket and trying to smile.

"I'll talk to you. The town's about half an hour west on the Turnpike, then north. I have no idea what the junior high school is like. But I just have to be there a month or two, right? If Karen comes through, I'll be attending high school where she goes to college. That should be OK, right?"

She had ignored the question about whether we would see each other. We had both lost childhood friends who hadn't moved more than a mile on the other side of town. When they changed daycare, changed elementary schools, they might as well have been swallowed up by a black hole. We never saw them again. Kelly and I both knew we were standing there, kicking pebbles into that very same black emptiness. Even if I saw her again, everything would be different. It was already different.

"Oh, yeah. For sure! Schools in towns with big universities have to be good. They have professors' kids going there and all." I smiled at her, about to burst into tears again.

She blinked, looked away, and then hugged me again. "I should get going. I'm going to miss you,

Elizabeth Freeman. Don't take any shit off of Cynthia. And if you see Wolf... if you see Daniel, give him my love." She knew I probably wouldn't see him. But I think she needed me to know that she was thinking about him, too.

"I'll miss you, too. And I will. I'm sure he misses you." I took hold of her shoulders and looked her in the face. "You haven't done anything to be ashamed of, Kelly Nash. You're gold. OK?"

"OK," she said, turning and opening the door to the car. "I'll call you in a few days and give you my new telephone number and address." She turned back toward me. "Beth?"

"What, Kels?" I was biting my lips, trying not to cry again until she pulled away.

"My aunt is going to tell my mother about my dad's affair. Think it will make a difference?"

"Not one bit."

"Children's Zoo?"

I laughed. "Definitely Children's Zoo."

She smiled, shook her head, and gave me a small wave as she got into the car and closed the door. Her aunt paused just long enough pulling out of the driveway to let the street sweeper pass. Then the car sped away. In a few minutes, Kelly would be driving past Wolf Boy's woods. "He won't even know," I thought. "He won't ever get a telephone call." Then again, I wasn't sure I would either.

CHAPTER 31

Time passed. Days stacked up into weeks. I had gotten one call from Kelly. She was doing fine at her aunt's house. She was finishing out ninth grade at a school there. She said that the people seemed nice enough, but she was convinced that teachers and guidance counselors are the same wherever you go. I told her what I could about her old school and what people were saying about her sudden departure. I wanted to make it sound more dramatic than it was. The truth was that people stopped talking about it after only a few days. Kelly didn't ask about Daniel so I didn't bring him up. I think we both felt him there, not talking in the silences.

It was maybe a week later. I had finished my homework and was in the living room watching a crime drama with my mother when the phone rang. I jumped, but didn't get up immediately. Without

Kelly, I was getting far fewer telephone calls and virtually none at this time of night.

"Beth, could you get the phone? I have my hands full." My mother was still knitting the sweater she had started last December.

"Hello?" I was expecting it to be a call for my mother. If it was a man on the other end, was I supposed to pretend it was a business call?

"Beth? Hi. It's Eric. You have a minute?"

I hadn't thought about Eric since Kelly left town. Which was odd since I know he was there at school, even in some of my classes, every day for all those weeks. I just hadn't noticed him. I felt guilty and Eric had no idea I felt anything at all.

"Oh, hi Eric. What's up?"

"I just saw the weirdest thing. I heard the dogs barking next door and went to the front door to see if there was a raccoon or something in the yard. But it wasn't a raccoon. It was a guy about our age, maybe a little older, walking down the middle of the street."

I didn't get it. "OK, yeah. I guess that's a little weird. Maybe not spectacular. But why are you…?"

"Beth, this guy was walking down the street yelling for Kelly."

CHAPTER 32

I know Eric heard me gasp. My mind was buzzing. Daniel. The town's Wolf Boy was out roaming the streets where people could see him. That was not a good thing at all.

Eric kept talking. "Over and over. He just kept yelling the name Kelly. I mean, it could be he has a dog named Kelly and she ran away. Or maybe there's someone in high school named Kelly and they had a fight and she got out of his car. I don't know. But there was something about how he was yelling that name. I had this feeling that he was looking for... well, your Kelly. Kelly Nash."

"Oh, crap. Oh, crap. Let me think. Shit. Yeah, you were right to call me. I think I know who it is. Did you see which way he went?" The only word anyone has ever heard Wolf Boy say and he's screaming it in the streets.

"He took off down my street and turned toward Birch. I think he's probably closer to your neighborhood by now. You live between my house and Kelly's street, right? Do you need me to do anything? I can meet you…"

"No, that's OK. Thanks, Eric. You did the right thing calling me. I'll explain it to you sometime, I swear." I needed to get off the phone.

"No problem, Beth. Be careful."

"I will. Goodnight, Eric." I hung up the phone. I ran to my room for my sneakers and then back out to get a jacket from the hall closet.

"Mom, I have to go out for a while. I'll be back."

"Beth, what's going on? Where do you think you're going? You know you can't go anywhere this late on a school night."

"Mom, I have to go! A friend of mine is in trouble and I need to find him right now!"

"Elizabeth, you take off that jacket and come sit down here and explain to me what's going on. Who was that on the phone?"

"That was Eric from school. He was just calling to tell me about Daniel, a boy I know. He's a friend of Kelly's and mine. And I need to go find him and talk to him, right now. He's out wandering the streets looking for Kelly. She's gone and he doesn't know that. I need to tell him, make him understand what's happened." I was standing in the living room doorway. I was not taking off my jacket or making any movement to sit down.

"Beth, don't be silly. This boy must have already heard about Kelly. And if he's out there being crazy about her leaving town, it doesn't have anything to do with you. "

"No! That's just it. Daniel couldn't have heard about Kelly leaving! He doesn't know what's happened! And he needs to hear it from me. Mom, I have to go. Now." I slapped the side of the door.

"Oh, Beth. People leave all the time. If anyone knows that, it's me. I'm sure this boy will understand it without you going out after nine o'clock on a school night."

"Mom, this isn't about you. Daniel gets being abandoned as much as you do, believe me. This is so different."

"Ben didn't abandon us. He died."

"And Daniel's… father didn't abandon him. He died too. This is different. To Daniel, this looks like Kelly left him without saying goodbye. That's not how it was. She wouldn't have…" I was getting too upset and wasting too much time arguing. "Mom, I'll be back soon. I'll be fine. I won't go far."

I turned and made for the front door. I was out in the cool spring night before she could put down her knitting and try to stop me. I saw her at the door as I walked quickly down the sidewalk to the nearest intersection. I stood on the curb at the corner under a streetlight, wondering what to do.

A car drove by. I turned away so that the headlights wouldn't blind me and I wouldn't be able to see down the street. I hoped there wouldn't be more cars coming along. I wouldn't be able to hear anything if there were cars. The tail lights disappeared as the car rounded a corner at the bottom of the street where the neighborhood emptied out onto Maple Street.

It got quiet. It was too early in the year for crickets and we didn't have any bodies of water nearby, so there weren't even any spring frogs — the peepers my cousins always told me was a sure sign of spring. This night was very quiet except for the dull white noise of cars on the turnpike. That hardly counted since, in my experience, that sound was always there.

I turned in one direction, then the other. I listened. At first, nothing. But then... there it was. I heard him in the distance. I heard a voice I had never heard before but still a voice I knew. It was yelling and yelling for Kelly. Eric was right. Daniel seemed to be heading in my direction.

It hurt hearing him this way, thinking that he hadn't spoken in how many years, that he had never once spoken to either me or Kelly. And now, here he was, screaming out this one name. It must hurt so bad. It must hurt more for him than it did for me and I couldn't comprehend how that was even possible. Again, I looked one way, then another. I wanted to make absolutely certain I knew approximately where he was. Kelly. Kelly. He didn't stop. He wasn't giving up. Kelly.

I wasn't sure my idea would work, but it was the only idea I had. Instead of going to where I thought Daniel might be, I stayed where I was, my ears locked on the sound of his voice. He was much closer now than he had been. I would only get one decent chance at this, so I waited until I was worried he might get past me if he was on the next street instead of mine.

"Daniel!" I yelled his name as loud as I could in the direction of his voice. I waited five seconds and then yelled, "Daniel, come here!"

Call it a hunch. Call it an educated guess. Call it the last desperate act of a girl who was so wildly out of her depth. But I thought that, if I could hear Daniel calling out Kelly's name and have a general idea where he must be, then Daniel — who was experienced in both surviving in the woods and in navigating the town in the dark — could find his way to me just by following the sound of my voice. Yes, only yelling his name twice was handicapping him a little bit, but I was optimistic and borderline romantic. He could do this as easily as I could find loose quarters at the bottom of my mother's purse when I needed gum money.

That was all I could do. I felt that if I yelled any more, a neighbor would come out of his house or someone would call the cops or my mom. I thought I could still make her out standing in the open door of our house, eight driveways and two streetlights up the street. I listened. Not a sound. Just a truck horn on the highway.

Then I heard it. I heard running footsteps. And of course I could hear them from over a block away because Daniel only owned the one pair of boots. He had never stolen a pair of Converse. I looked down the street and saw a shape dart through one streetlight's patch of light. Then it moved through the next one, this time recognizable as a human runner. I knew it was him. When he got as close as the nearest streetlight, I quietly called to him.

"Daniel! Over here. It's me. Beth." Why did I have to identify myself? How many girls did he know who called him Daniel? He slowed down and came to a stop a few feet from my curb. He was wearing only his jeans and a flannel shirt.

"Kelly?" His voice was low now, gentler than I ever imagined it would be. The way he said Kelly's name wasn't simply a question. It was like the sound of ripping your shirt to shreds before falling to your knees. It was a question, but it was also a huge stew pot full of grief and hunger and desperation.

"I knew you would hear me," I said. "I would have tried to find you, but I didn't want to go too far from home this late. I live right over there," I said, pointing to my house up the street. I realized that I had no idea what to tell him, so I went with the truth. "Daniel, Kelly isn't here anymore. She isn't at her house and she isn't even living in this town. She had to go far away. She isn't coming back."

"Kelly." I couldn't see his face, just glints of light from the streetlights, reflecting off his wet eyes. He said her name again. "Kelly."

"She would have stayed if she could. She would have stayed with you and with me. But things got bad for her at school and with her parents at home. She had to leave or else… she might have died." Did I believe that? Yes. Something bad would have happened if she hadn't left. "Isn't it better to know she's somewhere else but OK and happy? She didn't want to leave. She had to leave. She still loves you even if she's not here."

I wanted to hug him. Kelly hadn't meant to hurt him, but she did anyway. Meaning to or not, people damage each other. I reached out a hand toward him in the dark, but he was already gone. He had quickly turned around, vanished from the edges of my streetlight's patch of orange, and started running away, back the way he came. I watched for him and listened to the sounds of his feet hitting the pavement. He ran faster and faster, disappearing without ever saying another word.

CHAPTER 33

I heard the first sirens at around midnight. I was upset and couldn't sleep, so I was lying in bed, staring at the ceiling. That's when I heard the first fire truck. Then I heard another, followed by either a police car or an ambulance, maybe both. They were faint, so I went to my bedroom window and opened it. My window didn't face anything except another house, so there wouldn't have been any way to see lights or anything. But I wanted to hear what was going on. There were so many sirens!

After a few minutes, the sirens faded. I left the window open and got back into bed. I must have dozed off a little while later. When I woke up a little before two, my room smelled of burning wood. There was no going back to sleep after that.

That was the night the forest between the turnpike, the highway, and the turnpike on ramp burned.

More specifically, a small, rundown building deep inside the woods caught fire, igniting nearby trees.

The fire was first spotted by a truck driver passing by on the on ramp. He smelled smoke and saw a glow from inside the woods. He called for help on his CB radio. Fire trucks came, and then more trucks as the first trucks did not have enough lengths of hose to reach far enough into the trees to put out the fire, which was still burning two hours later.

At dawn, after the fire was out, firemen and police discovered a suspicious pile of stones near the charred remains of the shack. Additional police and crime technicians were called to the scene. The rocks were moved and two human skeletons were recovered from the grave. One had been dead perhaps ten years. The other had been dead even longer.

The shack that had caught fire had been inhabited until very recently, but there were no signs of the person or persons who had been living there. It was in the news for a week or so and then people forgot about it, even the bodies. The autopsies said they died of natural causes. Everyone moved on.

I didn't know any of this the next morning as I left for school. I only had a sick feeling that the burning smell in my bedroom wasn't a good thing. I closed and locked the front door. And there it was. As my screen door closed, I saw something blue on the steps. I knew what it was before I bent over to pick it up. It was a disposable Bic lighter.

CHAPTER 34

It was mid-May. For the first time this year, there were men mowing the grass in front of the Municipal Building. The leaves had burst onto the trees two weeks ago and now the trees lining all of the town streets were a vivid, psychedelic green. Flowers bloomed. Robins hopped across sidewalks from lawn to lawn. I had waited for spring for so long that it was almost impossible to believe that I had made it through winter to see it. It was bright and the sun smelled fresh.

It was hard to say whether a lot had happened in my life lately or nothing at all. School would be ending soon. The ninth graders were taking a bus to the high school next Tuesday to get a tour and meet the principal and vice principal. The eighth graders had already gone on their tour. After that, there would be the Farewell Dance to get through, then the actual junior high school graduation. Both the dance and graduation would prove to be too many people. The dance would degenerate into a food fight between classes. Graduation would be held outside and drag on for hours as people became sunburned and younger siblings began crying from boredom.

But those things were yet to come. For now, I was sitting on the bench in front of the Public Library. I had just been inside, trying to find something light to read for the next couple of weeks to take my mind off of classes, high school, Kelly, Daniel, and all of the adults in all of our lives. I found a couple of novels that were nowhere near up to the task, but I decided I didn't want to waste any more time looking. I was on my way to the Front Desk to check them out and leave. I was walking past the Reference Room when I heard Ms. Dornan call my name.

"Beth! Do you have a minute? I found that information you were looking for."

She waved a large manila envelope at me. She handed it to me with a questioning look. I did not open the envelope in front of Ms. Dornan. If she already knew what was in the articles inside or if she had guessed why I had wanted to know about the Whitmires, she didn't say anything. I thanked her for her help, checked out the two books I had picked out, and then walked outside into the bright spring sunlight.

To recap... it was mid-May. I was sitting on a wood and concrete bench in front of the Public Library. My two disappointing library books were sitting on the bench next to me. And in my lap, I was holding Ms. Dornan's manila envelope. I weighed it in my hands. I turned it over and ran my fingers across the clasp. I folded open the metal clasp wings

— and then I folded them back. Did I really want to do this? Did I really want to know?

I had called Kelly after the fire and told her what I knew. I told her about the lighter and that I was sure Daniel was still alive. I was almost certain he had set the fire himself and run away. She said she hoped he would be all right and then she changed the subject. I couldn't tell whether Kelly was upset. I think she would have been if she had allowed it, but somehow she couldn't. Put it in a box and put it away. She was trying hard to concentrate on her new life and moving in with her sister. I can't say I blamed her. She said she would come to my graduation, but of course she didn't. I didn't blame her for that either.

I took a deep breath and opened the envelope. Inside were several sheets of paper — photocopies of articles from the local newspaper. Ms. Dornan must have been able to find these on the old microfiche copies. The articles were paper clipped together. Ms. Dornan had stuck a Post-It on the first page. On it was written, "Hope these are what you were looking for." I'm not sure what I'm looking for, I thought.

A better question might have been "what was I expecting to find?" Since the fire and the discovery of two bodies at the shack instead of just one, I hadn't known what to think. Before that, I had expected to learn someday that Daniel had been living in the woods with his father, a draft dodger from the Vietnam War. I realized that I'd made up this story under the influence of my own family's experience. But the timing made sense and I couldn't think of another reason for an adult to purposely run away to the woods with his son.

The state police forensics lab wasn't expected to release their results — including possible identification of the bodies — for another six months. It wasn't a priority; no one suspected foul play. What the local sheriff's office had told the press soon after the fire was that the skeletons were of a female and a male. The female had died many years before the male and the male had probably been dead at least 5 to 7 years. That meant Daniel had been alone since he was around 11 years old. That he didn't want to talk, even if he knew how, wasn't surprising.

The first article was a small piece, perhaps from some sort of "Goings on About Town" page. It proved me both right and wrong:

Town Welcomes Soldier Home

Lifetime town resident, Lt. Clay Whitmire, returned home yesterday from a second tour in Vietnam. His bus was met by his parents and Lt. Whitmire's fiancé, Becky Mills, of nearby Henderson. When asked of his plans, Lt. Whitmire said, "It's just good to be back in civilization. I want to find a job, maybe in carpentry." The couple expects to wed in the fall.

So Daniel's father did serve in Vietnam. He wasn't a draft dodger. If Clay Whitmire was Daniel's father, then being good at carpentry would explain how well the shack had been built and kept up. He would have had to haul wood in at night, maybe park a truck on the side of the road, dump the wood down the embankment, then come back and drag the wood into the trees and down by the stream later. He could have built the shack in the daylight. But that would mean he planned to leave... that he built the shack before they ran away. And by "they" I meant both Clay and Becky.

The second article was a bit longer, clearly from the front page this time:

Area Family Missing

Police are asking area residents for any information they might have on a missing couple and their toddler son.

Clay and Becky Whitmire were last seen two weeks ago at Krogers. Their car was found abandoned along a road two miles north of town. The couple was first reported missing by Becky Whitmire's parents, Mr. and Mrs. Robert Mills of Henderson.

A search of the Whitmire's apartment showed no sign of a struggle or foul play. There was also nothing at the apartment that suggested the Whitmires had gone on an unexpected trip. Police believe some of the couple's clothes are missing, but the majority of their belongings are still in the apartment, including all of the child's toys.

Police Office Dale Reardon briefed reporters. "We're hoping that they didn't go on a hike with the little boy and get lost in the woods. That sort of thing happens more often than I'd like to say. Most of the time, we find people before anything bad happens to them. But people break legs and can die from exposure if they are out there long enough. I don't like that it's been this long without us having any word on their whereabouts."

Robert Mills told police that he didn't know of any reason why his daughter and her husband would leave town without telling anyone. Clay Whitmire had worked at Lucas Building as a carpenter until being laid off

> four months ago. He is a Vietnam veteran.
> Becky Whitmire was an athlete in high
> school. Their son is two years old and has
> dark hair.

I read this article a second time, and then a third. This was frustrating! It raised more questions than it answered. So I assumed that this is when Daniel's family ran away to the shack in the woods. Clay Whitmire had built the shack in the woods between the highways over time. He might have even kept it a secret from Becky but, if he did, she went with him anyway when it came time to disappear. I had to think she was in on the plan all along. Why would she do that? There's no mention of Clay's parents in this article, just Becky's. What did it take for her to just disappear with Clay and Daniel one day, leaving her parents behind, her friends, her past?

The third article was an obituary for Clay's father, Martin Whitmire:

> **Martin Whitmire**, aged 66, died on Tuesday
> at Mt. Auburn Hospital in Nelsonville. He is
> survived by a daughter, Mindy Whitmire
> Johnson, her husband William, and three
> grandchildren. He is also survived by a
> brother, Carl Whitmire. Mr. Whitmire was the
> husband of the late Gladys Simms Whitmire,
> who died in 1973. Graveside services will be
> held at the city cemetery on Saturday at
> noon.

There was no mention of Clay, Becky, or Daniel (whatever his real name was) in the obituary. I wondered whether Mrs. Whitmire's obituary mentioned Clay, coming much sooner after his disappearance. Or had the family just written Clay and his family off entirely? If I somehow found Clay's sister, Mindy, what would she say? If the state police weren't able to identify the skeletons as Clay and Becky, should I call them and make an anonymous tip? What would Daniel want me to do? He would probably want me to hold my tongue. Of course he would.

When Eric found me there on the bench and said hello, I had been sitting and thinking for going on half an hour. I had put the articles back in the enve-lope, folded over the flap, and reopened the metal wings. Then I put the envelope under my two library books and immediately and completely lost track of everything. I was staring at the grass, the trees, the people rushing past in their cars. Everywhere there were these faces of kids and adults, men and women. There was no way to imagine all of their stories. There was no way to know how they hurt each other or saved each other, every hour of every day.

I looked up and saw Eric standing there. He was smiling, holding three books of his own. "Mind if I sit down?" he asked.

I smiled. "Hi, Eric! No, I mean… sure. Have a seat." I had seen Eric around school since Daniel disappeared, but I hadn't paid him much attention. I felt guilty about that. Not that I was paying much attention to anyone at school since the fire. I just wanted school to end and for summer to begin.

"Have you heard from Kelly?" he asked me. He was sitting on my left with his feet on the ground. He hadn't put his books between us. He sat right next to me, his leg maybe three inches away from mine. Our elbows almost touched.

"Once or twice. She's moving in with her sister in a couple of weeks. She'll be OK." I looked over my shoulder at Eric. He had started shaving. His eyes were perfect just the way they were.

"The guy that night? The one who was yelling for Kelly? You said you would tell me about him." He looked me in the eyes.

No, not now. "I will, Eric. Someday I will. You just stick around and keep asking, OK?" I smiled at him and looked away before I could get embarrassed. I could see not waiting until senior year.

We sat there for a minute, not saying anything. The green of the grass in the midday sunlight hurt my eyes. Squinting, I asked him, "Eric, are your parents normal or are they messed up? I've been thinking lately that they're *all* messed up. Every single one of them."

He laughed. "I don't know, Beth. You could be right. On the other hand, they probably thought their parents were pretty messed up, too."

I thought about that. "Maybe. Maybe."

A car drove up to the curb. It was my mother. She was there to pick me up. "Eric, could you wait a second?" I took the envelope out from under the books, folded it, and stuck it inside the front cover of the first book. Then I picked up the books and trotted over to my mother's car. I gave her the books.

"Mom, can you take these home for me? It's a pretty day. I want to walk home after all."

She looked past my shoulder at Eric and gave me a look. "OK, just don't run off," she said. I waved as she pulled away, then walked back over to Eric.

"C'mon, mister. You're walking me home. And we have a long way to go."

 C ⋅ 8

About the Author

Andrew Amster was born, grew up, and generally survived a conventional upbringing in Lexington, Kentucky — though not in the 80s. He has been a geologist, a teacher, an online curriculum developer, and a writer/editor of assorted science educational doodads. He is the father of two [insert gender and species here]. He claims to bear no resemblance to Mr. Witherow. Then again, he claims a lot of things.